GIANT

GIA

NT

a novel

AGA MAKSIMOWSKA

PEDLAR PRESS | Toronto

ACKNOWLEDGEMENTS
The publisher wishes to thank the Canada Council for
the Arts and the Ontario Arts Council for their generous
support of our publishing program.

LIBRARY AND ARCHIVES CANADA
CATALOGUING IN PUBLICATION

Maksimowska, Aga, 1977-
Giant / Aga Maksimowska.

ISBN 978-1-897141-47-2

   I. Title.

PS8626.A4246G52 2012   C813'.6
C2012-901423-0

COVER ART JT Winik

DESIGN Zab Design & Typography, Toronto

TYPEFACE Adobe Garamond Pro

Printed in Canada

THE CANADA COUNCIL | LE CONSEIL DES ARTS
FOR THE ARTS | DU CANADA
SINCE 1957 | DEPUIS 1957

ONTARIO ARTS COUNCIL
CONSEIL DES ARTS DE L'ONTARIO

To my family, but especially
Sabina Kosznik
and
Maria Maksimowska

There is nothing worse for mortal men than the vagrant life, but still for the sake of the cursed stomach people endure hard sorrows, when roving and pain and grief befall them.
— Homer, *The Odyssey*, Book xv

The Laughing Heart

your life is your life
don't let it be clubbed into dank submission.
be on the watch.
there are ways out.
there is a light somewhere.
it may not be much light but
it beats darkness.
be on the watch.
the gods offer you chances.
know them.
take them.
you can't beat death but
you can beat death in life, sometimes.
and the more often you learn to do it,
the more light there will be.
your life is your life.
know life is your life.
know it while you have it.
you are marvellous
the gods wait to delight
in you.
   — Charles Bukowski

PART I

ONE

THE FOUR OF US are gathered in the hallway, the only place in our apartment the sun cannot reach. My grandmother, Babcia, wears a stained apron over her work clothes. A slip peeks out from underneath her striped polyester skirt. She has agreed to exit the kitchen for precisely one minute.

"The new generation always outgrows us old farts," she says, a touch of annoyance in her voice. She tugs at her gold wedding band and amethyst engagement ring, places the rings in my little sister's palm. Kasia cups them, baby birds fallen from their nest. Does Babcia think she'll measure up more without her rings? Back-to-back with Babcia, Dziadek levels a pencil across our heads, his hand unsteady. Kasia stares, her mouth falling open. Dziadek peers over his reading glasses with the same concentration he uses for threading a needle.

"Yes," Dziadek says, "you are officially taller." Dziadek is an official kind of man, so I take his verdict as gospel. Although he's a Communist, he's an honest man. People listen when the retired Director of the National Bank speaks.

He writes *Małgorzata, August 14, 1988*, beside the mark he makes on the wall. One hundred and sixty-nine centimetres. I am not yet eleven and I'm a giant. And I'm Gosia, not Małgorzata.

I step away from Babcia.

"You've grown taller than Lech Wałęsa," she says.

"That's not difficult," says Dziadek.

Babcia ignores him. "Soon, you'll even outgrow your Goliath grandfather. Can I get back to work now?"

When Babcia cooks everyone is banished from the kitchen. While Dziadek measures Kasia, I spy on Babcia. She pounds meat into thin slices, hides pickle and onion inside the slices and rolls them into tidy packages, which she pierces with toothpicks. At the sink, she peels potatoes with a soldier's speed and drops them into a cold-water-filled pot on the stove. Each one lands—splash—explosive detonated. When she starts making *makowiec* I retreat onto the balcony with my notebook. When Babcia bakes, she *becomes* the kitchen: cupboards slam, counters vibrate, flour billows, her arms flail. The outcome is different each time. Instead of being grateful, Dziadek grumbles. He says she spends money they don't have—no one has—on baking supplies and delicacies, frivolities instead of necessities. Then they argue about what's necessary, she deflects an insult or two while he gets something 'unnecessary,' like a handful of prunes, thrown at him.

We live in Morena, a suburb of Gdańsk, without our *mama* or *tata*. Tata divorced Mama and moved out five years ago, and Mama left for Canada more than two years ago. Morena is near the Baltic, which we cannot see, although seagulls visit our tenth-floor balcony. Dziadek says that seagulls are flying rats: garbage-picking vermin of the sky. I think they look like swans—graceful but aggressive, going after what they want. This is how I'd like to be, if I could shrink myself by half. In school they tell us that Morena goes all the way back to the ice age—*a moraine*—a glacial mountain that stood majestically above the port city of Gdańsk and fed it fresh water.

There are countless other housing developments like ours all over Poland and in the Soviet Union. Morena is about as special as a stray cat. Our apartment block is constructed of concrete slabs, a sixty-five-unit house of cards joined together with school glue. Dziadek is the one who got us this apartment, thanks to his spectacular bank connections. Mama says he got it for us so we wouldn't live in his two-room flat with him and Babcia—pickled herring in a teeny jar, like most other families in Gdańsk. Dziadek says that Morena is an up-and-coming neighbourhood. "It's a Communist apartment-block suburb," Mama used to say whenever Dziadek praised it. To me she would add in a whisper, "You'll see: we'll get our own place one day, one that's not a Soviet bunker."

The Germans, who ruled the city for longer than the Poles or the Soviets, used to call our city Danzig. Dziadek looks German, with his ghostly blue eyes and white hair, although he swears he isn't. In 1943 he swore he was, and that's how he got out of Stutthof, the concentration camp on the Baltic coast. Stutthof is why he refuses to peel potatoes, even though Babcia says peeling potatoes is men's work. During the war, Gdańsk was The Free City of Danzig, but Mama always says "So much for freedom. The war is over." Now the Soviets sort of rule Gdańsk and the rest of the country, even though Poland is a separate country on the world map. We're a satellite state, a puppet in the hands of the ventriloquist USSR. The Soviets have many puppets, other satellite states like us: Bulgaria, Czechoslovakia, East Germany, Hungary and Romania. Babcia says the Soviets—who Dziadek calls the Bolsheviks—are murderous and tyrannical, but not as much as the Germans. Dziadek says, "The Nazis killed civilians who were not German citizens, whereas the Soviets killed mainly civilians who were Soviet citizens, so you tell me who is more tyrannical?" When Babcia says, "Are you *defending* Hitler?" he rustles his newspaper and pretends to read, or calls her a Bolshevik. She grew up near the Russian border. Babcia has blue eyes, like Dziadek, but hers are darker—navy—and her hair is brown, speckled with silver.

Tomorrow is my eleventh birthday. Terrible things happen on and around my birthday, especially when we're here, in Morena. Birthday celebrations are usually held at Babcia and Dziadek's, in Oliwa, another suburb, a beautiful, old and leafy one, but Babcia says it's time to have a birthday in our own apartment, the first and last time. But I don't know why she says "last time." Maybe she means that when Mama comes back we'll have big family dinners in Oliwa, with all the aunts, uncles and cousins, like before. Maybe when Mama comes back they'll stop ignoring us and decide that Mama's divorce is not actually "immoral," as Mama's brother once said. Maybe when Mama comes back she will get us a nicer apartment, and we won't live in ugly Morena anymore.

I WAS BORN ON the Assumption—August 15—a Catholic feast devoted to the Mother of God. When I was eight, Mama explained to me that unlike Jesus, who used his own powers to get to Heaven, his mother had to be hoisted up, or assumed, by the muscle of God. "But I don't need anyone to give me a boost," Mama said.

Babcia peered from under her wild eyebrows and landed her fist in the middle of a ball of yeasty dough. It deflated. She was making my favourite *pączki,* doughnuts she fries twice a year: for Fat Tuesday and for my birthday.

"Religion is the opiate of the masses," Mama said.

Babcia snorted. "Where did you learn that?"

Mama just stared her down while Babcia said to me, "We're lucky to be able to celebrate the Assumption."

I am still confused. Dziadek is a Communist, and he goes to church sometimes. Yes, he has to wear a wide-brimmed hat and stand outside in the churchyard during most services. But he participates, waving assorted tree branches on Palm Sunday and blessing hard-boiled eggs on Easter Saturday, allowing black dust to be deposited on his bald spot on Ash Wednesday and seeing Jesus born at Midnight Mass. It's true: he doesn't do Catholic parades—no Corpus Christi marches in June, or Stations of the Cross on Good Friday—only Party parades are acceptable.

"Will the Communists forbid my birthday party?"

"They can forbid things all they want," Babcia said. "They can murder priests and put the fear of God into people, but Poles will still be faithful to their Father." She tossed the dough into a ceramic bowl and covered it with a tea towel. "It needs more time," she said. "Everyone out of the kitchen."

SINCE BABCIA'S BEEN LIVING in our apartment, juggling two households, living like a gypsy, she has neither the time nor the resources to make for me the celebration she wants. "Your mother has no proper implements in this kitchen," she says, exasperated, rummaging through cupboards full of soup pots and cake pans. "How did she ever cook for you?"

"Why won't you make pączki for my birthday?" I whine. "You don't need special implements for pączki."

She looks at me, studying my chest and belly with her invisible measuring tape, assessing my need for deep-fried sugary treats. I know the real reason Babcia won't make pączki is because it's been a wet year, not because I'm fat. She does nothing but fatten us up. It's been a rotten, washout of a year. Poor harvest. Rotten fruit in drenched trees. At the start of the third year of my mama's absence, there are no plums, no time to dry them into prunes and cook them down into plum butter, hence no plum-butter doughnuts.

"Go on, read on the balcony," Babcia says.

I grab half a loaf of stale bread. Dziadek will eat bread that's as blue as Danish cheese, he will eat it until it grows legs and walks away from him, another Stutthof side effect, whereas Babcia prefers bread straight out of the oven. She admits that fresh bread is bad for your tummy, but mint tea makes the ache go away and hot bread is the least of her vices. I head back onto the balcony where I summon seagulls with chunks of bread.

I know why our Communist-connections apartment was my anarchist mama's sanctuary. Had she continued living with the Tyrant Babcia and Comrade Dziadek, she would have murdered them both. Mama said that our *blok* on Piecewska Street is named for a female comrade. Piecewska is the road that leads to old Gdańsk. Gdańsk became a city in 997—before the Lenin Shipyard built massive boats, before silversmiths hammered amber jewels into shape—which makes it nine hundred eighty-nine years old. I hope not to be here when Gdańsk turns one thousand. Piecewska Street has a modern Catholic church, the long path to the church somewhat obstructed by shrubbery, and a bus route into town. During sugar- and television-free Lent, we walk along the path to the church every single morning while it's still dark, carrying lit candles, cardboard funnels shielding the flames from the wind, motivated only by the promises of Fat Tuesday. Under Babcia's watch, it's a consecutive forty days of church attendance.

I don't have to wait too long before the seagulls come. They descend like hail to the bread I've lined up along the balcony railing. They don't stand in line like stupid people at the grocery store, waiting in front of padlocked bars for anything the authorities might dump on them should they be moved to: toilet paper, butter, cooked ham. The gulls grab and go, their beaks upturned. How sly they are.

"Małgorzata!" I hear my full name, but it's not Babcia. "So much ruckus!"

Our neighbour, Pani Kowalska, my friend Beata's mother, is hanging laundry on the adjacent balcony. She's shouting at me but I can barely hear her over the greedy birds. "They'll shit all over my sheets." She waves her arms about. "Don't bring them here! They're parasites."

"I don't bring them. They just come."

"They wouldn't come if you didn't feed them," she says, and snaps the wrinkles out of a clean tea towel. "We get one loaf a week per family and you're wasting it on *them*?" She snaps the towel again for emphasis. "A sin."

I don't say anything; I just stand there, a knock-kneed oaf.

"Well?" she says.

I shrug and hand her the bread through the partition between our balconies. She puts the remainder of the loaf under her arm and takes it inside with the empty laundry basin. Tomorrow morning, she will feed hunks of stale bread drowned in hot milk and sugar to poor Beata.

It is deadly quiet. Everyone must be at work or away on summer vacation, or a combination of the two, like Mama and Tata, because the streets are as empty as if the Pope were in town. I hang over the balcony like a rag doll, the railing jammed up my armpits, legs limp. The urge to hurl myself over is lessened in this position. This apartment is on the top floor, which is actually the eleventh floor, not the tenth, because the ground floor is called *parter,* floor zero, not floor one. Polish people have a lot of trouble starting at one. It's always nothing first. Why not start with one? Start with *something* encouraging instead of starting with nothing. It would be quite the fall if I jumped.

Sharing the top floor with us are two other female-headed families. There are the Kowalskis and the Kwiatkowskis: the blacksmiths and the florists. Babcia has invited them to my birthday party tomorrow, but I think it's stupid. She thinks I won't notice that Mama's siblings are not here if she puts the Kowalskis and the Kwiatkowskis in their chairs. Divorce is commandment zero in Poland: thou shall not leave your husband or your wife. Leaving for a while is good; leaving for good is bad. Leaving your children with the grandparents indefinitely? Wait and see.

All fathers on this floor work at sea, on massive container ships carrying train cars and cranes to and from Asia. Ours is the only divorcé. The men are at sea—that's where our tata is right now. He is the only one who doesn't sleep here when he's on land. But like the other men, when he is in the city he sits in the living room and drinks, so it is like none of them is ever home anyway. Tata has worked at sea since before I was born. He went to night school after he met Mama. Mama is the only person in our family with a university degree. Tata calls himself an engineer, but I know he's not. Our surname—Wasiljewski—is carved on a lacquered piece of wood that is nailed to our front door. Dziadek wants to remove it, but I won't let him. We're still here. Our functionally named neighbours can tell we are Russians from way back by our surname. At least it ends with a –ski, "like all good Polish names," Dziadek says, because his has the same noble ending, Jankowski, whereas Babcia's is a peasant name, Mazur. Like Wałęsa. Regardless of our names, our neighbours treat us with the same disapproval we show for the Brechts, who live on the ground floor. The Brechts are the kind of people who don't write the Wise Men's initials K+M+B above their name plaque on the day of the Epiphany with chalk blessed at church. The names Kacper, Melchior and Baltazar don't mean anything to them, so we ignore the Brechts, like Babcia taught us. She says they're heretics. Dziadek says they're Jews. Whenever we used to walk past their apartment with Mama, she'd chastise my sister and me for being rude. "We can pray to foreigners whose names are not Polish, but we can't casually bow and say good morning to neighbours who are different?" I don't pray: praying scares me. It summons spirits, and I don't like things I can't see with my own eyes. Whenever the elevator breaks and we have to climb eleven flights, we come across a swastika drawn in the stairwell. "Jesus Christ!" Mama said, the first time we saw it, and fished a pen from her purse.

BABCIA COOKS WITH a wet dishtowel on her shoulders. Her blouse hangs off the back of a chair. Multiple straps criss-cross her back: brassiere, slip, apron. She says hell is this hot. Nobody's outside. I'm sweating like Dziadek when he weeds the garden in July. The railing under my armpits is slick with my perspiration.

There was record-breaking heat the final summer Tata lived here, too. The usual cool breeze off the Baltic had gone missing. There was almost zero reprieve. A bunch of people fainted during the Corpus Christi parade and an old lady in our building died. Mama wouldn't let me march in that heat, which made Babcia seethe with anger. But my grandparents always avoided Morena when Tata was home, so the seething was done from afar. I went to Oliwa for sleepovers while Mama taught private English lessons for extra cash and had get-togethers with her Bridge-playing and Leonard Cohen-worshipping friends to keep her sanity.

Tata spent the hot days watching Lechia Gdańsk soccer matches and European track and field competitions on the new television he brought home from Taiwan. Mama prepared for her lessons in the spare room. Beata Kowalska said it was a ridiculous TV and that her black and white Zenith made movies look much more romantic than our *nouveau riche* behemoth. But she's just jealous because Tata is a machinist who can hide things in the belly of the container ship, whereas Pan Kowalski, the ship cook, can't. Smuggling things onto the boat from ports abroad can get people in trouble. One time, two guys with guns forced their way into the Kwiatkowskis apartment. They have one son, Piotrek, who is really stupid and is in my class. Pani Kwiatkowska had a gun stuck to her head by goons who Dziadek says were looking for the drugs that Pan Kwiatkowski smuggles home. Pan Kwiatkowski is a machinist, like Tata, but there is less danger in televisions than there is in drugs.

The *nouveau riche* behemoth made Tata happy. He talked in funny voices and let me have sips of his cold beer. The beer bottles were so big I had to hold them carefully with both hands and concentrate while I tilted and sipped. When a beer bottle was empty, Tata would blow into it and make loud foghorn noises. When I'd try, I'd only spit on myself and Tata would laugh. Mama would sometimes come into the living room and shush us. "I have a student in there," she'd say. Her belly grew fatter and fatter each day. "Can you keep it down please?" Tata would get up and turn the TV down and I'd hide the beer bottle behind my back and nod.

"And stop giving her beer," Mama would say, her back turned to us.

"Beer is better for her than cigarettes are for the baby," Tata called after her.

She'd respond to that with a slam.

"Make her quit smoking, Gosia. She smokes like a shipyard worker, like your grandmother."

Babcia is not a shipyard worker; she's the provisions manager for all the grocery stores in the city. That's why we have more food than food stamps allow.

As my fifth birthday approached, it got hotter and hotter. The empty beer bottles were a tower in the kitchen, and the cigarette butts piled up in Mama's Union Jack ashtray in the spare room where she now slept. Tata stayed in the living room. All parents sleep in living rooms, except for mine. That's another of the many reasons why I'm such a freak. Mama let me have a kitten to keep me company while they jousted and the sun baked Morena bone dry. Beata found the black and white kitten in the garbage chute between the ninth and tenth floors, in a box with six others. I guess the box wouldn't fit through the chute door. The kitten was tiny, the size of Mama's palm.

I gathered sand from the sandbox to make up a litter box. A Doberman came sniffing around the kitten and me as I was scooping up the sand. The dog grabbed her and tossed her violently, back and forth, by the neck, until she succumbed. Blind with tears, I walked up eleven flights of stairs because I didn't want the neighbours to see my mangled kitten. Tata tried to console me, and said there will always be more kittens. This was the one time I prayed. I took my kitten down the path to our church, carrying her in the cardboard litter box partially filled with sand. Would the priest bury her in the churchyard? I thought maybe the angels would resurrect her. But the priest said no. "The churchyard is not even for people anymore."

ON AUGUST 14, 1982, the day before my fifth birthday, Mama stood in the middle of the square hall at the centre of our apartment in her leather slippers. Tata stood in the door to the living room, his feet pale and sickly against the wooden floor. Their raised voices had turned my attention away from the new mural I was drawing in my room. Mama had ripped the wallpaper off one wall and painted it white. The wall was for me to draw on, which meant I was forbidden from walking around the apartment with my crayoned hand rigid, marking my territory with strokes of red or green. Years later, I would use the same technique to gouge my father's fancy car with my house key.

As their fury increased, I stood on the threshold of my room, digging my fingernails into a warmed red crayon. Mama looked as if she were possessed. I had never heard her shout so viciously. Mama's pregnant belly jutted out in front of her, a kind of shield.

"But you bought the TV for this apartment," she said, her eyes darting from Tata to the television behind him.

"I bought it for *us*," Tata said.

"Then leave it for *us*," she shouted.

"Thanks to you, there is no *us* anymore," my father yelled. "He can bring his shit here if he wants to, the goddamn fool."

"Who? No one's bringing anything here," Mama said. She stood still, her feet rooted, although I could have sworn she swayed from side to side, a weeping willow. Tata disappeared into the living room and said from within, "I'll have everything out by tomorrow." Sports trophies and photo albums landed in suitcases like bricks.

I went into the hallway. "But tomorrow is my birthday party," I said, placing the shrunken crayon in my other hand and wiping the toxic colour onto my shorts.

My mama was the only one who heard me. "There'll still be a party," she said, looking at the spot where Tata had stood. "There'll still be a party."

But there was no party. Mama never finished baking my cake. The batter stood on the kitchen table, abandoned, the red gelatine for the top layer setting in the fridge. When I woke in the middle of the night, it was raining, a first reprieve from the insane heat wave. The rain came down hard and the clamour of it on the corrugated tin windowsills made it difficult to sleep. Mama was calling my name. Tata was gone. She was sitting on top of the toilet lid with her legs spread, blood the colour of my wax crayon spilling haphazardly on the tiny black and white tiles. "Gosia," my mama said. "Call the ambulance. The baby is coming."

I knew to call 999. I'd witnessed an ambulance being called many times when neighbours knocked on our door in the middle of the night. My mama resented "the Communist clowns" but Dziadek's Party favours always came in handy.

The ambulance took Mama away. Babcia stayed the rest of the night with me. She cleaned up the bathroom while I slept, and Dziadek came over the next morning with fresh buns and a newspaper. He wished me a happy fifth birthday and kissed me on the eye instead of the forehead. We went for a walk but didn't visit Mama in the hospital because only the husband was allowed to visit.

After a few days Mama brought home the premature Kasia. Kasia's skin was translucent as communion wafers and her head was flat on one side. She screamed and screamed and screamed. Babcia said the baby was colicky. I threw my pillow into her crib to shut her up. I left it there on top of her face, just long enough to feel guilty. When I lifted the pillow, the baby looked like she had died in mid-whistle, her tiny lips purple and pursed. What prevented me from peeing my pants from shock at the sight of a murdered baby in my room were the laboured breaths escaping her flared nostrils. I poked her, too hard, in her belly until she squirmed, and went back to bed once she started crying again.

TATA PICKED UP his last load a few days after Mama's return from the hospital. He brought me a small red plastic umbrella with white polka dots. It looked like the Smurfs' mushroom house. It was packaged in soft plastic that smelled like all Made-in-Taiwan things he brought home from his trips, except for the TV, which came in Styrofoam and cardboard. "Happy birthday, Małgosia," he said, and rubbed my hair. He showed me how to open and close the umbrella. It broke on his third try. "I promise to bring you a new one next time," he said, and chucked it. It was ridiculously tiny for a five-year-old as big as me, but I nodded.

Tata chose the ideal time to live elsewhere, peacefully, away from a colicky baby and a cranky kid. When my kindergarten teacher sent home notes about my picking fights with boys and exposing my underpants while climbing trees in the schoolyard, Tata wasn't the one to sign them. Later, when I refused to vacuum my room, he wasn't the one to drag me across the carpet. When I drew up an adoption certificate for Kasia, the bad-omen baby who stole my birthday, he wasn't the one to explain why it was hurtful, to discipline and finally to comfort me. In my own defence, I know very well that it was hurtful.

TOMORROW KASIA will be six and I will be eleven. Maybe we're finally old enough to meet whatever comes. Because whatever it is, it's probably bad. Someone must be going away, because no one is coming back. Maybe Dziadek has finally had enough.

Maybe Babcia is tired of juggling two households. My theory is that someone will make a dramatic exit.

Mama says I should stop theorizing and start reading. When I started school she forced me to read every afternoon, a half hour each day. The bulbous kitchen timer was set—tick tick tick—maddening—I stared out the window for the first fifteen minutes. Eventually I read. Each sentence took a full turn or two of the minute hand. The first time around, letters tumbled in my head like bits of glass and beads in a kaleidoscope. The second time through, the letters and words usually fell into place, although some remained hidden and confusing. Attempt three worked, if I didn't start doodling in the margins by then. I got through a paragraph by the time the alarm went off.

Babcia continues the reading torture. She says, "You won't even read your mother's letters," to which I say, "If she has so much stuff to tell me she should come home and say it to my face." I refuse to read Mama's letters. Babcia reads me bits out loud, but I usually zone out. This makes Babcia crazy. She punishes me by setting the reading timer to one hour.

I've been working through the same book, *Gulliver's Travels*. I can sometimes relate to Gulliver, in Lilliput, for example, surrounded by pesky, squabbling midgets, but the giants in the Brobdingnag part are pretty stupid. I don't want to be a scholar, like Mama. I'd rather be an athlete, like Tata. I'm smart enough to know that it makes no difference what I want: there are no overweight athletes. So I will be neither an athlete nor a scholar. A Polish nothing is what I will be.

Mama is always reading, except when she is typing or marking. She sits in the living room, smoking, reading thick leather- and cloth-bound books. "This is good stuff," she says to no one in particular. She says "Jesus!" or "bullshit" or laughs hysterically while reading student papers.

Or at least she used to. One day Mama was reading *Quo Vadis* while Kasia played with other kids in the sandbox out back, Pani Brecht watching from her ground floor window. Mama sat on the brown couch with her tanned legs outstretched and her perfect bare feet propped up on the coffee table, my brown-haired mama sitting on our brown couch against the backdrop of patterned brown and beige wallpaper, brown dishes with brownish poppy-seed cake sitting atop the brown coffee table with the brown glass tabletop, reading a brown leather book while sipping steaming brown tea out of a brown cup.

"What is it about?" I asked.

"It's a love story," she said, picking a piece of tobacco from her tongue and flicking it away. Her nails were shiny and red, oval, not bitten for once. "Set during a time when a great tyrant ruled the Roman Empire. Everything was his way, or else." She looked at me carefully with her feline eyes, like I was to remember her words. She must have meant a tyrant like Dziadek when he was just a father, or tyrants like the Germans when they were Nazis. "He persecuted Christians and waged war against the Jews."

"But lots of people have done that," I told her. This is one of the few things I had learned, albeit not at school.

"But did they also kill their own mothers and siblings?"

I thought about this. That's a horrible thing to do, even if your mother is nasty and your sibling is trouble. "That Quo Vadis was a bad guy," I said.

My mama smiled, put her cigarette out and reached to rub my head. I deflected her hand with my elbow. I hate head rubbing. It turns my hair into a ball of wool. "Nero," my mama said. "*Quo Vadis* means 'Where are you going?'"

Lately, I've thought about this question often. The only answer I can come up with is that I am nothing going nowhere.

A FEW MONTHS before my ninth birthday, Mama took the train to Warszawa. Warszawa has a star over it in the atlas, like

Berlin, Bonn, Kopenhaga, Moskwa and other capitals. It's nice that in the atlas, at least, a Polish city is as good as any other. She said she was going on business, which was strange, because her business has always been in a high school in Gdańsk and occasionally at the University, not in the capital.

When Mama came back, everything was swift and furious, no dawdling. Apartment organized, bags packed, cupboards stocked, plans made. She said she had an opportunity that would be a shame to miss. That it'd just take a few months; that she could make more money in those few months than working for years in Gdańsk. "When someone gives you something," she said, "you take it. You don't say no. No matter how you feel about it. In Canada, they pay in dollars."

Dollars: which meant the rest was as obvious as if you were a man from Gdańsk who has no job in the shipyard, is not in the Party, or in the church, or clever enough to be a doctor, lawyer, or tradesman—you earn dollars on container ships.

Dziadek drove Mama to the airport. The new car he had been waiting for since retirement, the Fiat 126p, also called *Maluch,* Little Guy, because it's so tiny it's a miracle it doesn't get squished by trucks and trams, was idling in the drive. While the *Maluch* was sputtering and coughing downstairs, I had one final opportunity to quiz my mama about her strange opportunity.

"Where are you going?" I said, standing between her and the front door.

"I already told you, *pączek,*" my mama said. I hated when she called me doughnut. "To work, in Canada, to make some money, so we can have our own place."

"We already have our own place."

I didn't understand why she needed to leave. Lots of people left, escaped Poland for good, took their children with them, people who didn't have well-connected fathers and had to live with their in-laws, crammed into tiny, telephoneless, pre-war apartments by the train tracks. One of Mama's cousins had loaded up his Lada with leather jackets, furs and homemade spirits, and sped off for the Czechoslovakian border en route to Austria during the curfew days of Martial Law in 1980-81. Mama had countless friends from her English Studies university days, mostly women, who got jobs on cruise ships or at trade fairs, journeyed around the world, married foreign machinists, manufacturers, merchants, and stayed in random places forever after: Rotterdam, Sztokholm, Adelaide, Chicago, Neapol, Kopenhaga, Londyn, even Tokio. But Mama always said those people left because they had nothing. She has a lot.

"Can't I come with you?" I said.

"What about Kasia?" my mama said.

"What about my first communion?" I moaned. It was coming up in a month and it was essential that Mama be here for it.

"I can't take you with me," Mama said, "not yet."

I pretended not to hear the last part. "Kasia's much too little," I said. "You don't have to take her. Take me. I'm big enough to work."

"It won't be long," Mama said to me. "It won't be long— you'll see."

My mama has a funny idea of what long is. And I can't see long, although I sure as hell can feel it, stretching and pulling inside me as if my guts are being wound around rusted spools.

She left our Gdańsk-Morena apartment with the same haste as Tata, gone in a mad dash. She must have prepared for it, trained hard and practised. Everything that fast is slow in planning. An earthquake that takes seconds to wreck everything is a result of billions of years of slipping and shoving of tectonic plates. Those plates have no choice but to live side by side, often on top of one another. They hate this setup. They push each other around, siblings vying for the top bunk, to the point of eruption, ruin and exhaustion. After the quake: calm. A sad empty calm, with too much time to think, to wonder about ridiculous things.

WHEN I CLOSE MY EYES, I see Mama standing in front of a small class of girls. No boys anywhere. She looks smart and neat. A wraparound plaid skirt secured with a large silver pin hugs her curves. She wears a white blouse with a giant romantic ruffle and a pearl necklace. Each pearl is round and perfect, exactly the same as the one next to it. Her hair is up in a twist, effortlessly pretty with wavy wisps framing her face. She talks to these smiling girls, who are all really the same perfect blonde girl multiplied ten times, talks about all the books she's read, about ancient Rome and politics, about poetry and English phrasal verbs, writing and reading. When her lecture comes to a close, the girls stand and clap. Mama leaves the classroom, her patent leather heels clickety-clacking, a slim leather briefcase in one hand and a stack of books in the other. She doesn't have a free hand to wave goodbye to her admirers. But it's not necessary to wave goodbye. She will return in less than twenty-four hours. So instead, she looks back over her shoulder and gives them that sweet dimpled smile of hers, the one that fills you with certainty that everything is and will be okay and you are marvellous. Once she exits the classroom, her students will not pour out into the schoolyard and light cigarettes. They are Canadian. They know how disgusting smoking is. Instead, they stay in the classroom talking about their new teacher, an impressive import from Europe. I open my eyes when the sting of hot jealous tears makes it too hard to keep them closed.

Mama's been gone for twenty-eight months, which is over twenty percent of my life. I don't want to write stupid letters, although I will draw pictures at the bottom of those that Babcia writes. In her letters to us, Mama says, "Gosia: write to me. I want to hear from <u>you</u> how you're doing." I guess my pictures of ladies in high heels, kittens, houses with billowing smoke, puffy clouds in the sky obstructing smiley face suns don't convey the truth. I flip through my notebook of drawings and doodles. I wish I could stop being stubborn and write a whole book for my mama, a book that she would enjoy reading as much as *Quo Vadis* and *1984*. A book that would be her favourite novel: historical fiction with a touch of dystopia. She says dystopia is when everything is bad: the government, the economy, the mood of the people. I won't have to make any of that up. She will have to come back to read this great novel because it will be written in Polish and the authorities won't let it leave the country, much less have it translated into English. But, the chances of me actually writing a novel are as slim as I am not. How am I supposed to engage in tasks as simultaneously active and relaxing as reading and writing when my whole immense body aches from all this damn thinking and wanting?

TWO

KASIA KISSES MY FACE, leaving small wet marks on my cheek. "Happy birthday," she whispers. I reluctantly open my eyes. She has climbed down from her top bunk and is under the covers beside me. Her skinny five-year-old body is cool. Her skinny *six*-year-old body. "Happy birthday to *you*," I say and roll over her, delivering a full-body hug.

"Ow," she squeals. "You're going to kill me!"

"That's all I have to do to kill you?" I ask playfully, and together I roll us off the bed.

"I love you," Kasia says.

Members of my beloved band Europe regard me from the poster I've pasted across the slats of the top bunk. The frizzy-haired lead singer, Joey Tempest, watches over me. I like having him there.

"Shut up," I say and throw a pillow at Kasia. *What's there to love?* I feel hot and mushy, like oatmeal, and suddenly have the urge to cry. Then I harden a little, but I'm still hot. "I'm not making you breakfast today," I bark, "not on my birthday."

The living room couch has been tidied, the bedding stowed away. Babcia is already at work, in one of the grocery stores she supplies. Dziadek spent the night in Oliwa, as always, where he tends to his plot of city garden and putters around his garage.

"*I* can make *you* breakfast," Kasia says, pausing in the kitchen door. Her pyjamas are loose. There is an iron-on Smurfette on Kasia's concave chest: Smurfette's blue hands are clasped in excitement and she's levitating, white high heels dangling above a squiggly patch of grass.

"If you want to do something for me," I say, "go get dressed."

Kasia takes a running start and throws herself at me, reaching to wrap her skinny arms around my bum. The biggest part of me. Her hands meet at my lower back. She succeeds in encircling me and breathes, "Happy birthday," right into my ribs. She bounces off me just as suddenly, and scurries out.

Crying in the kitchen doesn't make me feel any better. It doesn't release any of the feeling of someone holding me by the neck. Why isn't Mama back? She said one year, then two. Has something bad happened? I open the window and scatter bread on the windowsill. The seagulls come in seconds, swarming, their squawking an orchestra of bicycle horns. They peck each other's heads. More bread makes the ruckus noisier. "Happy birthday!" I yell into the humid air and throw a handful of rye upwards like vulgar confetti. "Happy birthday, you giant fucking freak!"

A nurse attending our class's physical examinations at school last year said to me as I walked into the examination room, "You're the largest girl in your class." I was topless and wore only my red underpants. In order to hide my chest from her, I bent over to rub my achy knees. "Your bones are growing so fast they hurt you," the nurse said.

What did she know about me just by looking at my blotchy red skin and matching underpants? I had had an accident in gym class. We were practising long jumps when I fell and banged up my knee pretty badly. The pain was vicious. The doctor said then that he didn't recommend any more running, jumping, or climbing, because of my patella, not my bones at all. Stupid nurse.

"You're the largest girl in your class," she repeated and put her violently sharpened pencil between her teeth. "If you keep growing at this rate, your joints won't hold up."

I nodded. What did she want me to do? I *am* the largest kid in my class. Did she think she was imparting new knowledge? Boy, girl or teacher, I am the biggest.

The nurse's name tag said *Magdalena Komar*. I didn't know much about nurses, except for their ease with needles and pinching arms when needing to stab you with a vaccine, but this one's name, derived from a prostitute and a mosquito, told me a lot about her.

"My tata is almost two metres tall," I said. "He used to be a decathlete. He holds the Polish record in the javelin."

She didn't reply. Instead, she reached out her hand and did the most unexpected thing: she pulled the elastic of my underpants away from my belly. She peered down and studied the contents. Dark, curly pubic hair. Sparse, but mine.

"How *old* are you?" She examined a handwritten ledger, tapping her pencil.

"Almost ten," I said.

"*August 15, 1977*," she read, and removed her glasses. She had two symmetrical red marks on her nose that looked like someone had burned her with a pair of tiny irons. She rubbed them. "You're *nine* and a half."

"You have stretch marks. See?" She went on, pointing to the white squiggly lines that covered my hip bones. I didn't know they were called *stretch marks*. I thought of them as lion-claw scratches from a previous life. I had some on the sides of my breasts, too, which I now covered with my crossed arms.

"You're overdeveloped."

I looked down at my feet. They were ugly, greyish. I wiggled my toes. "Maybe it's Chernobyl," I said, and shrugged. "Maybe it's the red stuff we had to drink afterwards," I added. "My grandmother said it was poison."

"Stable iodine," she said solemnly, and shook her head. "Everyone had to drink stable iodine afterwards, and we're fine."

I stood in the middle of the office, bare-chested and cold, hands jammed into my armpits. The nurse consulted with her colleagues. If she brings them over here to look into my underwear! I swore I would use her sharp pencil and spear her right through the heart. And I wouldn't be sorry.

When she returned, she weighed me, turned me, she prodded my breasts with her cold hands. "Have you had your period yet?"

"No," I replied, horrified.

"Good, good," she said, and wrote something on a prescription pad. She folded the paper in half and handed it to me. "Give this to your mother as soon as you get home."

"My mother is not here," I said.

Magdalena Komar gave me a teacher look, but I wasn't trying to be a smartass. "Well then, give it to your father."

I held the paper out for her to take back.

"Let me guess," she said. "Who *is* here?"

I shrugged. "Babcia. Dziadek."

"Give it to your grandparents then, as soon as you get home, please."

I took the prescription and thanked her, begrudgingly, complying with Mama's rules of good manners. Before pulling my school uniform on, I peeked at the folded piece of paper. *Premature sexual development.* The word 'sexual' made my back rise into armour like an aluminum cheese grater. I crumpled the prescription as tightly as I could, squeezed my fist and chucked it in the first garbage bin I saw.

THE EVENING BEFORE Mama left, we stood in the kitchen among canned provisions and packed suitcases as she gestured warily with a sanitary napkin. "You're not even nine yet so this is premature," she said, and waved the pad around as if to disperse pesky flies. "You probably won't need this for a *long* time, but…"

Mama disclosed the secrets of womanhood to me that night: blood, cramps, mood swings. "You'll have to buy some more," Mama said, handing me the pad, "when you run out. Stamps allow one package per month. I'll leave one package for you behind the toilet. You do know where to buy them, don't you?"

"At the pharmacy," I said, holding the pad away from me at shoulder level, a paper airplane about to be launched.

Mama nodded proudly, as if she had just taught me something hard to master. She was sliding in and out of focus in the dim light of the kitchen. "No," I said, suddenly snapping out of my trance. I slapped the pad onto the kitchen table. Tin cans and dishes rattled. A crossword booklet slid to the floor with a slap. She looked at me, first bewildered, then sad. "I *hate* the pharmacy," I said. "It smells like sickness." Becoming a woman was evidently going to make me sick. A terrible disease.

I'VE HAD DREAMS RECENTLY in which I'm still a little kid and I'm swimming across the Atlantic towards Mama, starting in Rotterdam, like Tata does. If she doesn't come home, I will go to her. As I swim I grow heavier and heavier and drop to the bottom of the sea like a cannon ball. But I root my toes in the sand and the rest of me shoots up, breaking the surface of the water with a colossal splash. I am a true giant, a creature of fictional proportions. I take a huge step over the Atlantic, stretching my thick legs so far apart that I feel as if I'm going to rip in half.

Waiting for your mama is more infuriating than picking your kid sister up from school, or copying out a passage from the bible, word for word, into your Catechism notebook while the nun looks over your shoulder, or even getting hit on the palm with a ruler by that same nun because you default to writing with your left hand when you get frustrated. Mama will be surprised to see me when she comes back. People stare and whisper, trying to figure out the relationship between Babcia and me when we go shopping or walk to church: the old woman and the giant with a woman's parts and a kid's head. Piotrek Kwiatkowski from our floor calls me The Circus Freak, but never to my face. But he stutters and has to repeat the third grade, so he's one to talk.

Because Babcia's friend from work told her that the Communists inject chickens and geese with hormones to feed people more efficiently, she refuses to cook fowl anymore. Not even chicken soup with homemade noodles on Sundays. "It disfigures our children," the friend apparently said. Dziadek says that if he eats any more pork he will turn into a pig. "You are a pig," Babcia snaps, and pats me on the head like I'm her poodle.

BABCIA COMES INTO THE KITCHEN, weighed down by shopping bags full of loot. She deposits the cloth bags at my feet, as if I'm supposed to inspect them. "There," she says and kisses me on the cheek, last night's alcohol still on her breath. "The breakfast I am going to make for your birthday," she says. "Kasia!"

"I thought you were working today," I say, carefully extracting a brown paper bag of eggs from one of the shopping bags. The bottom of the paper bag is soggy. "You broke one."

"Oh, never mind," Babcia says and swats invisible mosquitoes with her hand. "I always break one. I was in such a hurry." She squeezes my face and kisses me again, greetings of good health and prosperity rhymed off between each peck of her wet lips. I wipe my face with my forearm.

If this moment were a cartoon in one of the illegal *ulotki* that Mama used to read (*Solidarność* flyers that smelled of celery root because they were printed with vegetable ink in damp cellars), Babcia would be drawn juggling eggs, also several kitchen utensils above a flaming stove. The way Babcia makes scrambled eggs makes me smile, although it grosses me out a little, too. She doesn't patiently melt butter, gently whisk eggs, slowly fry finely chopped pieces of chives and ham, like Mama used to. Babcia's scrambled eggs are an egg-butter-ham stew, the whites and yolks still separate entities in the finished dish.

At the bottom of one of the shopping bags, underneath a toddler-sized loaf of rye bread, a brick of white cheese and a litre of cream, is a soft package wrapped in butcher paper.

"Livers for my birthday."

Babcia scrapes the egg stew onto plates and sets the pan on an asbestos pad on the stove. Kasia waits at the table with fork and knife on end, a hungry pirate. She studies the package in my hands.

"Where's *my* present?" Kasia yelps.

I unwrap the parcel and register its contents. "Here's your present," I whip it at Kasia, "happy birthday."

Babcia sucks air in through her dentures, makes a disapproving whistling sound.

"Ew." Kasia lifts the flesh-coloured brassiere out of her lap with a hooked index finger. "Gross." She flings the bra at me.

"Can I have livers instead?" I say to Babcia. Surely she thinks me an ungrateful brat.

She is spending all of her free time with us. She could be gardening or saying the rosary. Babcia is an old woman who should be sitting under a blanket in a sanatorium, sipping funny smelling mineral water. We eat breakfast in silence. The odd hungry seagull stirs stagnant August air, waiting on our generosity.

A brassiere for my eleventh birthday. A butcher-paper wrapped brassiere from the farmer's market. Maybe Piotrek is right? People would line up to see a big fat pauper child with massive boobs in a tragic bra, flick coins at me and laugh their heads off. The only difference would be that they'd laugh out loud instead of snickering behind my back, and I'd get some of my own money.

WHEN PIOTREK KWIATKOWSKI asked me over to his apartment last year to help him with a geography project, I went out of pure boredom. His parents have an impressive boomerang hanging over their bed. His father—alleged drug smuggler—did a tour of the South Pacific on a tanker and brought back the boomerang, as well as a musical instrument that resembles a decorated elephant trunk. The Kwiatkowskis are the only parents I know who have an actual bedroom and don't sleep in the living room on a bed that has to be stowed away each day. I don't want to do Piotrek's homework for him. The last time he asked for my help I ended up drawing a comic strip for him for Polish class, earning him the top grade I wanted for myself.

"Why are we in your parents' room?" I asked Piotrek, who was on his hands and knees, searching for something under his parents' zebra-throw-covered bed.

"You like the boomerang?" he asked. "I think I'm going to do the project on Africa."

"Australia," I corrected. "What are you looking for?"

The window in the Kwiatkowskis' bedroom was carefully concealed by Venetian blinds and two layers of lace curtains that pooled on the floor like a bride's veil. The wallpaper in the room was loud: black, red and white embossed calla lilies. A photograph of Piotrek's mother hung in a red frame amid the calla lilies. She was posing seductively, her hands covering her nakedness. I was so transfixed by the photo of naked Pani Kwiatkowska that I hadn't noticed Piotrek resurface. He sat on the bed with a stack of magazines on his lap.

"Sit down," he ordered.

For some reason I did as he said.

He was breathing through his mouth, even though he was not stuffed up. His slimy little hand turned the pages of the first magazine, slowly, methodically, as if to give each of us time to register each forthcoming image.

Shiny legs, sharp nails, balloon breasts, pink nipples, puffy lips. My cheeks got hot and dry. I sat there, frozen, elbows tightly pressed into the tops of my hipbones.

"Look," Piotrek squawked.

I tried to defy him and look at Pani Kwiatkowska's portrait again, which suddenly took on the likeness of the Virgin Mary, but I couldn't look away from the glossy magazine pages for too long. Women who looked like real-live genuine and imitation Barbie dolls—wet and exhausted—extended over chairs, horseback, beaches and poolside, pulling apart their girl-parts and clawing at them with pink fingernails. One of the magazines had men in it, too. A couple doing something I hadn't ever considered possible. The man's boy-part was meaty and veiny, naked tree trunk without the decoration of leaves and flowers.

Piotrek grunted. "Sex. This is how babies get made. No storks anywhere, you see?"

Sex. That's how Kasia and I were made, Piotrek, Beata and all the other kids.

"I'll show you my penis if you show me your vagina," Piotrek said.

We sat so close to one another that the fine spittle of his stutter was spray on my shoulder. Vagina sounded like a diagnosis for a horrible disease, something old people get right before they die.

I stood up.

As if he were going to hug my midsection, Piotrek reached towards me and pulled down my sweatpants with one swift tug. They slid to my knees, underpants and all, my premature-sexual-development pubic hair centimetres away from Piotrek's fascinated face, exposed and available for study. I should have pulled everything back up before bashing Piotrek on the head with my fist, hard, because when Pani Kwiatkowska opened the door and saw me leaning over her small son reclining on the bed, me pantless, large and enraged, she yelped. "Get off him!" she screamed. "Get off him now!"

Sweatpants tugging upwards with one hand, pubic hair concealed with the other, I shuffled past her out of the bedroom. "You perverted, vulgar girl," Pani Kwiatkowska spat. "Preying on little boys. If your mother were here," she shouted after me. "You're like a grown woman, for God's sake."

IF MY MOTHER WERE HERE she would tell ignorant Pani Kwiatkowska that I am not a grown woman, though I look like one. Before she went to Canada and a few months before my first communion, I came home one afternoon after catechism class and kicked the shoe-rack in the hallway so hard that all of Mama's wooden clogs and high-heeled shoes and boots rattled.

"Why so happy?" she asked.

I grunted.

"Tell me," she said.

I flung off my fake, Taiwanese Adidas.

Mama dragged me into the living room and made me sit on the couch. She moved her papers off the coffee table and sat on it, right across from me. She could sit on the coffee table, being as slim and light as she is. She leaned into me with her hands on my knees, open grey eyes inquisitive.

"Sister Kinga says we have to order dresses through the church," I said, and I handed Mama the carbon copy of an invoice Sister Kinga had made up.

"No you don't," Mama answered matter-of-factly.

"We have to match, so *we don't look like the travelling circus.*" I made my voice all high and nasal to imitate my teacher. "Sister Kinga needs a deposit. And measurements," I said.

Mama and I knew this wasn't about shades of white.

"It looks like you care," Mama said and studied the purplish invoice. "Gloves? Rosary? Purse? Handkerchief?" she read. "Prayer book? Shoes? All of these things *have* to be white? *And* identical?"

I shrugged. "I know," I said. "It's stupid."

"You have a prayer book that I had to buy you at the start of the school year."

"It's black."

"And a rosary?"

"It's amber. From Babcia and Dziadek. You didn't buy it."

"And all these other things—couldn't you just borrow them?"

What neither Mama nor I were saying was that the nun's form excluded a child of my size from its inventory. The available items were designed for scrawny children, like Kasia, and Beata Kowalska. Even if my mama could afford the paraphernalia or wanted to spend her extra private-English-lesson cash on me, she could not outfit me properly.

I showed Sister Kinga's form to Babcia the following weekend, as soon as Mama dropped Kasia and me off in Oliwa. I told her what Mama had said.

"Nonsense."

She checked off the required items, including the nicest, most expensive dress. She gave me a wad of tightly folded red and brown bills to take to Sister Kinga. Mama found the form and the money in our room. She called Babcia and they bickered for a good half hour, saying some ugly things to one another. Afterwards Mama slammed the phone down so hard that Dziadek had to get us a new one.

Mama left for Canada shortly before my first communion, saying the timing was beyond her control. By then, ordering from the church catalogue was no longer an option. The deadline had passed. "I have an idea," Dziadek said when I cried about it. He disappeared into his garage and emerged with a box marked *Ewa*. He took an off-white dress out of the box.

"What's this?"

"Your communion dress."

"Don't make fun of me."

"I have no intention of making fun of you. It's your mother's wedding dress. I can alter it to fit you."

"But she was so skinny," I moaned. It was hot in the garage. Even my eyes began to get sweaty.

"No she wasn't," Dziadek said.

I knew Mama and Dziadek hadn't always gotten along, but calling my mama fat?

"This dress was made for you, too," he said, smiling and nodding, eyebrows lifted, as if I was supposed to complete his thought.

"What?" I gave up. I didn't understand what he was nodding at.

"For you. It was made for you."

"So I would wear it on my wedding day, too?"

"You could say that. It had to be cut a little wider in the waist to make room for you in your mother's belly."

I felt a little queasy. At the time, I knew that having babies before marriage was against God's rules. Dziadek was telling me that I was a bastard, a bastard without a first communion dress. A big, awkward, nine-year-old bastard without a first communion dress who was going to stand out from her classmates because of her inadequate frock and ample sin. Thank God I didn't know then, as I do now—thanks to imbecile Piotrek—that Mama and Tata had *sex* before they married. Gross.

Dziadek did set me up with a dress in the end, without any Party connections, without spending any money, without bickering and without breaking a telephone. And even though I sulked the entire sunny day because Mama had just left and I refused to be photographed by Dziadek, refused to carry the bouquet of miniature roses and baby's breath Babcia bought for me, and complained that the dress barely went past my calves, Sister Kinga said I looked lovely. I would never in a million years admit it to anyone, not to Babcia and Dziadek and especially not to Mama, but I was secretly pleased at the nun's compliments.

BABCIA ARRANGES A GAME of Solitaire on Mama's brown glass coffee table with the calm calculation of a priest handing out communion. She doesn't make her usual circus-magician snapping sound with the cards. The most recent bottle of cognac Dziadek received as a bribe sits open on the living room wall unit, a genie lamp waiting for someone to rub it, to draw happiness out of it. Dziadek still gets bribes, even in retirement. What can he do for people now? A shot glass of amber-coloured spirit glows by the reading lamp. Babcia inhales her cigarette smoke and holds it in her lungs; she requires more poison than usual tonight. I kiss her on the head, because I don't like the taste of nicotine and alcohol. She kisses me properly anyway and says, "I love you, *córeczko*." Every time she calls me her little daughter I feel hands choking me. I need seagulls to breathe, but seagulls don't come to fetch stale bread in the dark. "Do you want to read Mamusia's letter now?" Babcia asks. Even though I shake my head, she takes one piece of paper out of the envelope and hands it to me. "This one didn't come wrapped in plastic," she says. "Everything's here." This means that forty other people haven't read it before us, nosy government goons looking for God-knows-what in my mama's letters. There is a George Jetson sticker on the page, a red-white-and-blue airmail border, and mine and Kasia's names written in Mama's perfect handwriting. None of this makes me want to read the letter any more than I usually do. Babcia will write Mama after a couple of games of Solitaire and a few glasses of cognac, before she kneels to pray and before she sleeps. She will press hard on the graph paper, as if to make two or three copies of her words, copies that can only be touched, not seen. Her penmanship will turn from letters to waves towards the end and I will add my drawing to the bottom of the page in a day or two.

Babcia loves me too much. I can't ignore her birthday present even though the bra makes me feel like burrowing a nest in the floor of my room, turning into a potato bug, rolling in a tiny dry ball and staying there forever. The polite thing to do is to try the bra on. A grim task. Slipping the gummy straps onto my shoulders feels like blistering my skin with nettle. Babcia can't say I'm ungrateful, that she's the only one who makes sacrifices. I study my reflection in the tiny porthole mirror.

The bra fits, like Morena fits Gdańsk. My breasts are contained, lifted off my ribs, harnessed by the brassiere, but like Morena, everything also looks absurd. They jut out in front of me like they're no longer a part of me, but rather strapped-on baggage. The breasts are contained, yet somehow bigger than before. The bra will have a new home behind the toilet. Babcia doesn't get her period for some weird reason, so she won't think to look there.

I sit on the toilet and open Mama's letter. So many words. August 1, 1988. I touch their curly, embossed letters, press the page to my face and take in its grassy smell. It's almost like pressing Mama's soft, dry hand to my lips, sweet and warm like a plum-butter doughnut.

THREE

BABCIA HOLDS HER fingers in front of her face, moves them like snapping crab claws. "Lice," she says, "we were meant to pick lice out of each other's heads. We're meant to plant and gather, not sit around." She can be a little weird sometimes.

The last time Babcia said 'lice,' I was six and she was dowsing my head in turpentine. When that didn't work, she sheared me like a bleating lamb. She always has to be doing something.

"You need to move around. I'm an old woman and I lug bags around and hustle all over the city. That's why I'm so happy." She pauses. My babcia has a funny idea of happiness. "It's all this sitting around that's making you so—"

"Fat?"

"No!" She is theatrically appalled. "You're a developing woman, you're not fat. The sitting around is making you sad. Sluggish."

I don't know any women who are eleven and who like to play grocery store with their six-year-old sister and draw naked people in their notebooks and listen to Europe's 'The Final Countdown' eleven times in a row, dreaming of Joey Tempest. At school, Piotrek and the other boys tell me to get lost and go to the high school down the street, where I belong. But eleven-year-olds don't go to high school. Then again, people my size don't go to primary school, unless they're teachers, nurses, or janitors, so where do

I belong? It's not the sitting that is making me so sad, but Babcia does have a good point. I don't play outside as much as I used to. I've even given up climbing trees because my knees are so crunchy and my new body is so heavy. I'm tired of Morena, this concrete subdivision where the greenery is too short to provide shade. The only shade comes from navy blue militia vans creeping up and down the streets. I want the construction outside of Babcia and Dziadek's Oliwa apartment to be finished so I can play hopscotch with kids there who don't know that my mama and tata are gone. In Oliwa and the older parts of Gdańsk, there are fewer nooks and crannies where you can stumble on a militiaman landing his baton in the back of a teenager's knee, or a bunch of drunks holding an outdoor meeting with several opened half-litres of vodka.

Babcia swipes the stool from underneath me, forces me onto my feet.

"There's no one to play with outside," I lie to her. Our neighbours are here. "Everyone's away."

"Take your sister." She manhandles me out of the kitchen like she's pushing a wheelbarrow of cabbages through her garden plot. "Kasia!" Babcia yells, and Kasia instantly materializes in the hallway.

"Where's your leash?" I joke. Kasia punches me in the arm. She's strong for a kid. I rub vigorously, like Babcia taught me, to avoid a bruise.

I open the front door and Kasia leaps out, launching herself at the elevator button. "Ha! I got it."

The phone rings in our apartment as we're about to step into the elevator. There is a chance it could be Mama. I pull Kasia out of the elevator by her collar. "Ow," she yelps and smacks me one more time.

"Girls, wait!" Babcia calls to us. Kasia and I stand in the doorway while Babcia answers the phone. "I thought you said this evening," she says. It's not Mama. It's not Dziadek either because

Babcia hasn't said 'bloody' or 'idiot.'

"Don't go anywhere," she says after she's hung up. "Your father is coming to get you."

Kasia parks herself in the middle of the hallway to unbuckle her jelly sandals.

"He's your father and it's only decent that he should take you out once a year," Babcia says, fussing with the tea towel that's tucked into her apron. "It's his obligation. Now go wash up and put something fancy on. He'll say your grandparents neglect you."

Kasia and I both look down at our clothes.

Babcia is the queen of obligation: it's his obligation to see his children, it's your obligation to write to your mother, it's our obligation to go to Mass, say the rosary, confess, fast, see the Pope. I hate having to see people I don't want to see.

I puff out my lips and make the unhappiest face I can muster. Babcia pretends she doesn't see it. Stomping and grumbling all the way to the bedroom makes her at least follow me. She plops two preapproved selections on my bottom bunk: a polka dotted yellow tragedy and a striped maroon train wreck. This is not so that I will make a decision; it's a coercive tactic. I slouch across my bed on top of the clothes Babcia has picked out for me. Maybe if I wrinkle them under my immense weight I won't have to wear them.

"And hurry up," Babcia yells as she exits our room.

Last summer, when Mama was supposed to come home after her year-long contract was up, Babcia insisted that we go see the Pope, who was making a pilgrimage to his motherland. I had no desire to see this old man riding around a frenzied city in a glass bubble. I wanted to be left alone with my misery, my notebooks and some stale bread. When Babcia informed us of the Pope's arrival, Kasia shrieked, but I was not sufficiently excited about meeting the man whose photograph is displayed all over Babcia and Dziadek's apartment. There are no photographs of Mama or

Tata anywhere. Critical of my reaction, Babcia wouldn't look at me that whole morning.

John Paul II, *our* Pope, came to Gdańsk to visit with Lech Wałęsa. I wish Mama were important enough to visit with Lech Wałęsa. And because of the state visit I was supposed to be clapping and jumping and yelping as if Mama was coming home. Babcia said this was an extraordinary thing because together Lech Wałęsa and John Paul II would "throw the dirty Soviet Communists out, and then people would know that the only authorities oppressing them are their own." But Babcia hasn't even thrown out the dirty Communist who lives with her, so she should talk. Expecting Dziadek to swing at Babcia or say something horrible about Bolsheviks, I winced. He calls Wałęsa 'that peasant,' so I couldn't believe that he agreed with her. But to my shock, he also added, "It's time for Warszawa to act like the capital it is, not just an outpost of Moskwa."

"Here," Babcia said, and handed me the yellow polka-dotted frock with ruffles and a bow in the back. "I bought it this morning, at the market. It's beautiful."

It was revolting. It looked like cauliflower cooked to death, speckled with boiled larvae. What is it with Babcia taking the farmer's market for the mecca of *moda*? Hasn't she ever heard of a boutique? A clothing store?

"I won't allow you to go and pay your respects to the Holy Father looking like that!" She waved her hand at my Lechia Gdańsk soccer club t-shirt and worn gym class shorts. She was staring somewhere around my mid-section. "You should look like a girl for once."

In that moment Babcia took on the appearance of Nurse Magdalena Komar, pinch-nosed and humourless. An urge to snap the dress at her, as if it were a wet towel, made my teeth clench. "Stop oppressing me!" I shouted. I flung the dress on the couch.

The room went dead quiet.

Dziadek and Kasia looked our way with the same morbidity that's in all of our faces every time a militiaman approaches in the street and asks to see the grown-ups' papers. I never talk back to Babcia, except when she has had too much to drink and then it's like talking back to a stranger, so I suppose my outburst was a thing to see. An eclipse.

"I think it's all this heavy metal that's making you anxious," Dziadek said all of a sudden.

Heavy metal? Are you referring to the Europe cassette Mama sent in her first parcel? It's perfect. It's the soundtrack to the movie about my life, the one I play in my head all the time, the one that ends with Mama and me together at last. "It's not heavy metal," I pouted.

Babcia threw the dress back at me. I jumped. The frock's spiky ruffles grazed my eyeball. "Ow! Get away from me," I stomped, and hurled the dress on the floor. "You and this hideous *szmata.*"

"Szmata?!" Babcia shouted. She started to pull the dress over my head. "You ungrateful child!"

There was pushing and tugging and even a bit of slapping. No matter how big I get, Babcia always wins. The end result of our scuffle was a freak in a much-too-small jaundiced dress, a t-shirt with a logo visible underneath. So much of a standout was I that the Pope looked right at me from his glass Popemobile, picked me out from the Solidarność-flag-waving crowd, and nodded approvingly. Perhaps a Lechia Gdańsk fan, or maybe distracted by the enormous size of my boobs.

"Ready?" Babcia yells from the hallway.

I don't give a shit if the Pope approves of yellow ruffles. I get off my bed and chuck that dress aside. My other 'choice' for Tata's visit is a two-piece outfit, a present from Babcia's sister, Ciocia Fela, and the only fancy thing I have that fits. I hate fancy things. Ciocia Fela makes a living selling illegal merchandise—leather jackets, gold jewellery and clothing that she smuggles in from

Bulgaria and Czechoslovakia, at various markets in Gdańsk and neighbouring Gdynia. I pull the pink and mauve outfit on as slowly as I can, pretending I'm in my film and it's a slow motion scene. The slow motion slows down my heart, which thinks it's in a hundred-metre dash to break world records. Maybe Tata will get fed up and leave if I'm not ready, and we won't have to have a stupid visit. If he really loved us and missed us, he would live here, especially now that Mama is gone. We wouldn't have to have these obligatory visits. The horizontal stripes on the short-sleeved top and the vertical stripes on the knee-length skirt clash with one another. Chaos in Bulgarian cotton.

"You look like Babcia," Kasia says. She is swimming in my hand-me-down white dress with white embroidered flowers. It makes her thin limbs look tanned.

"You look like Dziadek."

TATA DOESN'T WANT to come upstairs, which makes my stomach rotate like the new bank-connections washing machine in our bathroom. The machine has a lid that I use as a shield when Kasia and I swordfight with badminton racquets. I feel rotten and nauseous, but if I say anything to Babcia she'll think I'm making it up to avoid the visit. While Kasia and I wait for the elevator, Piotrek Kwiatkowski emerges from his apartment with a mesh grocery bag. "Woohoo," he says and whistles, "going to the port to make some extra cash?"

"Go fuck yourself," I say. Kasia makes giant eyes at me.

"E-easy og-ogre," he stutters, "just paying you a compliment."

"Why don't you pay your mother a compliment and take a leap off your balcony."

Piotrek lowers his eyebrows and inhales, trying to prevent further stuttering. "Didn't anyone tell y-you you shouldn't wear horizontal stripes across your b-oobs because they look like t-t-tidal waves?"

I look down at my chest. The belly below it is decomposing from all the pain inside.

Kasia says, "Didn't anyone tell you you're a retard?"

I pull her by the arm and we take the stairs all the way down, our Made-in-Taiwan green jelly shoes slapping against the concrete that smells of piss and mould. I'm out of breath by the time we reach the ground floor, where Pani Brecht is unlocking the door to her apartment. She's dressed for church even though it's Saturday. "Good afternoon," Pani Brecht says, and bows. "Don't you girls look lovely." Her little girl Daria is with her, smiling sheepishly at Kasia.

Kasia, who is holding my hand, pulls me gently towards the door. My stomach feels like a sink full of dirty dishes.

"Thank you," I say. "We have to go now."

"You farted," Kasia says to me quietly as we walk out into sunshine.

Tata is sitting in his red car with one foot on the pavement, a race-car driver ready for photos. The usual suspects occupy the benches in front of the apartment. Tata and the louts watch us emerge from the building. We are in a Corpus Christi parade and they're the spectators, except we're not holding baskets full of flower petals that we can throw at them. Tata stands and opens his arms, wooden and large, the size of crucified Jesus above our church altar. "You're so big," he says, and kisses the top of my head, which comes just under his goatee.

"Tall," I correct.

He nods absentmindedly and squeezes my shoulders while looking at Kasia, who is allowed into his widespread arms and gets swallowed in them.

"I've missed you girls so much," Tata says. "Did you miss me?"

I nod my head mechanically (I should be made of metal and springs), and turn towards the car. The scratch I put down the side of it two years ago seems to have grown, an aggravated scar.

I thought I'd feel awful about keying it. It's kind of nice that he has to drive around with a reminder of me. Instead of moving in and taking care of us after Mama left, he said, "Your mother abandoned you. And for what?"

"WHY DON'T YOU TAKE the front," Tata says as I'm about to climb into the back seat after Kasia. "It'll make me feel less like a chauffeur."

No one ever lets me ride in the front. The front is for grown-ups. Plus, in the front you have to wear a seat belt that bisects your breasts like a road-sign arrow: look here. I shake my head but he says, "Come on."

"Where are we going?" Kasia asks.

"To the beach," Tata says, and turns the key in the ignition. "It's too nice out to do anything else." We usually go to the zoo or to the circus, but I guess the beach is as much of a spectacle.

Tata and I have the same thought at the same time. I know this because he turns off the engine and looks at me as I'm already unbuckling. "Małgosia," he says, "you better go get your bathing suit." Kasia doesn't have to run upstairs to get a bathing suit. I'm the only one in the car who can no longer swim in just her underpants.

ON THE WAY to the beach Tata jokes that we should turn off at Orłowo and go to the less populated nudist beach.

Kasia squeals, "Are you crazy? With *us*? We would have to see your penis then."

Tata laughs in spurts, like he's choking on dried sunflower seeds.

I have nothing to look at because both sides of the road are lined with mature trees and nothing else. My six-year-old sister has just said penis to our father whom she's met maybe half a dozen times in her life, three of which she likely doesn't remember.

My face swells and heats up. Tata looks ahead and changes the radio from station *one* to station *two* and back again.

WE ARRIVE at the municipal beach in Gdynia, which isn't far from Gdańsk, but might as well be in Canada when you have breasts and you're in the car with the father you haven't seen in nine months and your sister is talking about his penis. The beach is packed, crowded with families too poor to vacation in the lake district or in the mountains. "Does anyone work in this country?" Tata says too loudly. "Is this what Solidarność members do when they strike?"

I find an empty outhouse where I can put on my bathing suit. Thank God it's dark and mirrorless so my nasty nakedness can't stare back at me. But impertinent sunlight busts in through warped wall slats and forces me to see some of it: dimpled thighs oozing out of the suit's tight leg openings; soft belly distorting the flower pattern beyond recognition; sparse sickly hair growing beyond the area assigned to it. I close my eyes, inhale as deeply as I can, wrestle the short suit straps onto my shoulders, flatten my boobs toward my armpits as far as they'll go and count down from ten before taking this hideous body out to the peopled shore. Once there, I immediately jump in the water and swim out past the orange buoys that mark the life-guarded area, to get away from Tata and Kasia, from penises, breasts and vaginas of other people, which are as obvious and revealed in clingy spandex as mine must be.

Tata taught me to swim when I was a little kid. Dziadek applauded his no-nonsense coaching. "He's a seaman," Dziadek said. "He knows what he's doing." Tata had hurled me into the lake from the end of a rickety dock. I had been scared to jump, the black water ominous below. We were on holiday with Babcia and Dziadek in the Mazury region, which used to be Prussia. Mazury is the land of a thousand lakes. But lakes are not like the sea, they are lazy and they won't hold you up. If you're going to drown somewhere it will be in a Mazurian lake. But I didn't drown, I swam, swam a most frenzied dog paddle, right back to the dock. I grabbed onto Tata's toes and hung on tight, until he shook me off and I was forced to practise my dog paddle some more. As a result I am a pretty good swimmer. A giant like me should sink, but I don't. Whales don't sink, even though they're the largest living things in the sea. They are the largest, period. I used to marvel at how the container ships Tata works on stay afloat. Now that I'm so big I have a better idea.

When I finally crawl out of the water and cover myself with the two cheap towels Tata bought from a vendor at the beach entrance, Kasia and I build a sandcastle and dig a moat around it so deep that it fills with water. Tata is trying to construct a bridge over the moat, which I don't think is possible. Soon seawater will start eating away at the structure, the moat will get wider and the castle will collapse on itself. We will be left with a shallow soggy pit.

"I can swim thirty-seven lengths of a pool without stopping," Tata says.

Kasia's mouth is parted like when she sleeps on her back. "You can?"

"What kind of pool?" I ask.

"The pool on the ship."

"You have a pool on the ship?" Kasia asks.

"That seems kind of pointless," I say.

"We'll have to go to port and see it." Tata rubs Kasia's wet hair. It stands up like angry porcupine quills.

He's always drifting in the middle of all that water. No wonder he's such a good swimmer, so strong and athletic. If he had a Babcia to cook for him and a sister to go for ice cream with, he'd be fatter, like me.

Tata sifts sand from one fist into the other, a moving human hourglass.

"Do you still play sports, Małgosia?"

"Gosia," I correct him.

"Yeah, boxing," Kasia says. "She practises on me."

"This kid is a riot," Tata exclaims. More hair rubbing. "Your mother and I always played sports." The only sport I remember them practising was arguing.

"She was strong," Tata says. "You should have seen her forearms from all her sailing and volleyball."

I can't see her forearms, but I can see her hands, her long fingers with their elegant oval nail beds, the occasional nail bitten down, polish scraped like the peeling paint in my classroom. Those fingers, curled around cigarettes, pinched around pencils, laid out on typewriter keys, are now patting the smooth yellow strands of some Canadian girl's hair, pointing at her expertly written book report, the one with Mama's praise handwritten on top of it.

Sadness swallows me. Kids squeal, dogs bark, people laugh, waves break, but in my head it's all shhh…

Tata says, "Ice cream?"

I have a stomach ache, and the mention of ice cream brings up the *kiełbasa* and tomato sandwich I had for breakfast. But I'd rather eat too much ice cream that later I puke up than to keep wallowing in my pathetic sadness. He always gets us the number of scoops corresponding to our age, except in winter, when once we had chestnuts, but Tata is rarely here in winter. You can't buy ice cream anywhere in the winter. Babcia is appalled at Tata's waste of money. "Ten scoops?" she shouted the last time. "Did half of it end up on the pavement? Why doesn't he just take the money out of his wallet and throw it in the gutter?" Dziadek says Tata should take the ice cream money and add it to his insulting child support.

Although the ice cream scoops are small, smaller than ping-pong balls, eleven scoops on a single cone teeter like a stack of clowns on a unicycle.

"Let me help you," Tata says, and reaches for my cone.

"No," I protest, guarding the tower like a Lent candle with my other hand.

He grabs it anyway. "Just a little bite," he says, and takes half of it into his huge mouth. This is his method of ensuring harmony between Kasia and me.

Kasia beams, wagging her six-scoop cone at me.

Suddenly my stomach is doing somersaults again. Together with the ache it's a horrible, hollowing-out feeling. When I hand the rest of my cone to Tata he looks bewildered. He wipes his goatee. I have to do something to stop my stomach from ejecting itself right through my sunken belly button, so I crouch down and press my hands to the pavement. This makes the acrobatics in my stomach stop. "I need to go to the toilet," I say.

Seagulls start circling. Maybe they anticipate my cone being thrown in the sand, which it is. They pounce. All is quiet while they peck.

"Go with your sister," Tata says to Kasia.

The outhouse. An outhouse is better than bushes, better than sand dunes. But it's not a porcelain toilet with sanitary napkins hiding behind the tank. My body is turning itself inside out. I'm sitting on its wooden planks, never mind all the germs. Hovering above the planks is not an option, not with the twisting and the pain. My ears ring. Eeeee. I bear down with my feet against the outhouse door. Push. Kasia stands on the other side, her bare shoulders against the rough wood grain, a loyal Swiss guard, my toy soldier. Push. "Are you okay?" she whispers through a crack. I rock back and forth with my head pressed to my knees. The doctor Babcia took me to last year when I hurt my knee said, "You are so flexible, like a contortionist. Too flexible. Don't stretch too much. You'll hurt yourself without knowing and only long after will you feel the pain." Too flexible to build muscle, too elastic to develop strength. As he bent my joints back and forth, he also inspected the bumpy track-like scars on my knees, remnants of scrapes and falls. "Keloids," he said, "overgrowth of scar tissue. Be careful, because your body keeps permanent proof of all injuries. Your skin's memory is as good as your brain's. Sometimes they will throb like little heartbeats."

There is throbbing, and there are heartbeats. There is emptying. Back and front. I must be dying. When I start sobbing, Kasia repeats, more alarmed this time, "Are you okay?" I can see her small face through the cracks, her forehead and palms pressed to the door. "Do you want me to get Tata?"

"No," I blurt out, loudly, assertively. "No. Get me napkins, newspaper, anything," I say, and she's off.

The outhouse door opens. Sunshine floods in. I've summoned Mama. She's here. I am so naked. One-piece bathing suit on the disgusting floor, joining my ankles. But we've seen each other's nakedness, so she doesn't care about my grossness. Mama will take my face in her hands and she'll hold it like a ripe watermelon. She'll kiss me and clean me and give me soothing chamomile, and something stronger, from the pharmacy. And when I sleep the sickness away she won't go to a friend's house to play bridge. She will stay close, reading quietly by the dim living room light.

I look up from my rocking. A young woman in a fluorescent orange bikini shrieks and slams the door shut. I stand up, even though at any second I will tumble to the ground like a badly built tower of wooden blocks. But there's too much diarrhea, and blood, and so much dirt that I can't pull my swimsuit back up. I've been ripped apart. I'm dying because I miss Mama too much. My stupid monstrous body is breaking down.

There's a soft knocking on the outhouse door. "Are you still there?" Kasia whispers. I push the door open, only a crack. I don't want her to see anything. She's wearing my old white dress again. "No paper," she says, "but use these." She hands me her balled up, soggy underpants. "I'm all swimmed out for now."

AFTER I'VE SOMEWHAT cleaned myself up, I scurry out of the outhouse, wrapped in towels, my fancy ruined outfit underneath. Tata takes us home: the only blessing about my dramatic entry into womanhood is that it cuts our annual visit short. I can't see any other benefits to becoming a woman. When I get home, I will be really mean to everyone so they'll leave me alone, I will excavate Mama's pads from behind the toilet and sleep the rest of the afternoon away while Kasia helps Babcia prepare dinner. I won't bleed at night because nothing that happens during the day happens at night, and maybe tomorrow everything will go back to its own fucked up normal and I will be a beast child again instead of a useless woman.

FOUR

ON THE TABLE in front of Babcia and me in the Oliwa kitchen
is a metal pail full of wild mushrooms picked at Ciocia Fela's
cabin near the sea, brown and beige bits of grit-covered fungus
with specks of neon green moss that I rummaged for in the
debris on the forest floor. The only reason Ciocia Fela has a cabin
is because her husband is a Commander in the navy: young
conscripts built it for free. Dziadek always repeats that with a
sour look on his face. Nobody else has cabins. I hate having to
pick mushrooms, although I prefer them to blueberries, which
Babcia also makes us pick each summer. At least mushrooms
don't stain your fingertips purple.

Babcia hands me one of Dziadek's gigantic sewing needles, the
one he uses to sew suede elbow patches onto his cardigans, and a
spool of black thread. "Thread it for me," she says, "I've no patience."
I'm marking the last day of August by making a chain of wild
mushrooms. Their flesh is soft and gummy, almost human. I enjoy
sliding a sewing needle through their caps and stems. We're making
mushroom clotheslines to hang wall to wall, covering the entire
kitchen ceiling. They will hang there for weeks, shrinking into
blackish clumps, and we'll get used to their pungent scent and
their hovering above our heads like storm clouds. We'll take down
the chains by early October when they're good and dry and dusty.

"Let's save some for pickling," Babcia says.

I dump handfuls of mushrooms into a plastic laundry basin.

We dry and pickle everything. That's forward thinking. Babcia says Mama and Dziadek have none of this kind of thinking. We don't eat anything fresh, except the pastry Babcia bakes; we preserve things for much, much later, when we free them from a tightly sealed jar, which opens with a hiss and a pop. If the apocalypse comes, which it might if the government keeps murdering priests, firing teargas and keeping stores empty, our family will survive on mint, rosehip and chamomile teas, dill pickles, mushrooms, sauerkraut, pâté, horseradish, gooseberry jam, jellied pigs' feet, herring, kiełbasa and tripe. Kasia is on apocalypse duty, too. She and Dziadek are in Oliwa, at the garden plot, collecting the last of the cucumbers.

"I have a surprise for you," Babcia says.

I prick myself with the needle. My heart begins to eat itself. My hands tingle so much I can hardly hold onto the string of mushrooms. I have to open and close my fists several times to make the tingling stop. The last time anyone had a surprise for me was shortly before Mama's departure for Canada and look how that turned out. Is Mama finally coming home?

"Your mother," Babcia says, "sent money for school supplies."

Babcia beams and opens her hands as if to show me what a large fish she's caught. "You can buy whatever you want this year, even the fancy expensive paper."

My face must be grim grim GRIM because Babcia says, "You can buy paper with those blue fellas on it." I've been covering my school books in brown butcher paper, or sometimes scraps of leftover wallpaper, ever since I started school. I'm impressed she knows that Smurfs are blue even though they're grey on the television since Tata took the colour TV away. But I'm suddenly filled with overwhelming rage at Babcia, as if it's her fault that Mama is not coming home. As if she has done something to make

Mama stay away for so long.

I'll have to face another school year alone—Mama won't be here to help me stomach the horrible Russian language I will have to learn, to save me from the brainwashing with her smartass retorts to Babcia and Dziadek, with her insightful anti-Soviet comments. I could cover my Russian books with swastikas, see what Babcia says about fancy paper then.

THE MUSHROOM-CLOUD canopy is complete. I leave Babcia to smoke her cigarettes in peace. She kisses me and says, "Thank you for your help," and closes the door behind me. She doesn't normally thank me. I know she's doing it to lessen her guilt for closing the door, for smoking inside the apartment, for pouring herself a drink when it's still light out. For delivering such a terrible surprise. Hopefully Babcia won't have so many drinks that she starts bumping into things. I don't mind that Babcia needs time alone. It's Dziadek who minds, and he's not here right now. He'll mind when he's back from the garden with buckets full of stuff and there is no place to put any of it and Babcia is sitting on a three-legged milking stool in the middle of the kitchen singing folk songs and smoking.

I open the window in Dziadek's bedroom. This is where I often sit. Sometimes I peruse the atlas, but I'm sick of North America and the Atlantic, so I hang out the window instead. Even though a cool breeze is blowing in from the Baltic, high from the Scandinavian Arctic, and the hot humid weather has cleared, the bad birthday omens have not passed. Something bad will still happen. They're transforming into back-to-school omens. September first—the first day of school and the anniversary of the start of the Second World War—is tomorrow. We start every school year with silence, the school filling with melancholy, remembering how the Germans attacked us from the Gulf of Gdańsk on September 1, 1939, while the West sat on its hands.

There will be speeches from veterans and stories of destruction. We will stand in the schoolyard like little soldiers, dressed in our uniforms of navy blue and white.

Last year on the first day of school, Babcia told me the most horrible story I have ever heard. She was ironing the new, larger uniform Dziadek sewed for me, and not talking, which never happens. She was fixated on the dark fabric, sliding the iron right and left. One spot was wrinkle-free while all other areas were overlooked. Her guiding hand barely got out of the way of the devilishly hot metal sliding over the material. She frequently wears a nasty burn on her forearm or hand: baking, cooking, ironing, grating. "My father would have been eighty today," she told me. Was she crying? The steam in the iron hissed, popping as more steam shot out. Her face was flushed.

There weren't many stories of my great-grandfather, just photographs of a slim young man in uniform. I knew he had been killed during the war. "The Bolsheviks murdered him," Babcia said, wiping her forehead with a closed hand. "I wasn't much older than you are.

"In my nightmares I still see the blade slicing upwards, over and over," Babcia said. She continued moving the iron over my uniform. "I will never forget it."

I was sitting on the carpet, cross-legged: walking over to her, to pat her arm or kiss her forehead, was not an option. My legs were lead.

Babcia's father was an army man, but also the town butcher. The family was better fed than anyone else, and they shared what they had with their neighbours. "They hoisted him up by his ankles, like one of his cattle," Babcia said. I wanted to shush her, to scream 'Why are you telling me this?' I kept my head lowered, plucking hairs from my shin. Babcia was weeping, telling me her mother had tried to block her view of the gruesome sight, but little Babcia had already stepped into the blood that drained from her father. Her mother couldn't protect her. She failed.

"I can't protect you, I couldn't protect your mother," she said through tears. "And your mother can't protect you."

BABCIA OPENS THE kitchen door and yells to me from the hallway. "I'm going out."

I snap out of my daze and pull the window shut.

"Okay," I yell. I'm jittery all over even though I haven't been caught doing anything bad.

"Tell Dziadek I'll be back later. Yesterday's *pierogi* are in the fridge."

Instructions for dinner? "Where are you going?" I call.

"I won't be too long," Babcia calls back.

When all is quiet, I fall asleep on Dziadek's sofa, dreaming that I'm drowning, and growing, swimming towards Canada through cold, late-August Atlantic waters. Babcia is swimming alongside me. She isn't a good swimmer. Fish nip at our legs, there are explosions in the ocean that toss us around and kick up sand, rubble, pieces of ship wreckage. The whole journey is a mess. Babcia begins to sink and I panic because I think she's dying.

Babcia did almost die once. I was six. I knew something was wrong when Dziadek picked me up from Grade 0. Adults who weren't government officials, teachers or janitors rarely came to the school. We drove to Oliwa and ate a dinner of cold cabbage rolls and bread, just the two of us. Dziadek said, "Babcia had a heart attack." I couldn't breathe properly and couldn't finish my food. My tears fell to the plate, and finally Dziadek took it away, saying, "We'll go see her."

Dziadek's car, the *Maluch,* lived under padlock in the concrete garage, with gasoline jerry cans, clothing in bags loaded with mothballs, Mama's boxes and other things covered with sticky layers of cobweb and dust. Dziadek opened the door to his garage more often than he turned the key in the *Maluch's* ignition. He would disappear in there to get away from Babcia's angry cooking. In the garage, he invented garden contraptions, tools and gadgets to grow more efficiently his gooseberries and rhubarb, gadgets Babcia mocked as useless pieces of wood and wire.

The car coughed before reversing onto the pavement. I stood, waiting, on the drive, where the exhaust made me sick. Before I could clear the saliva collecting in my mouth, I threw up on the side of the car.

Dziadek drove nervously, his knuckles white on the wheel, his jaw tight, his eyes shifty in the rear-view mirror. I was sick once more before we arrived at the hospital, heaving at the side of the road.

We abandoned the car in a lot behind a demonstration of students carrying Solidarność placards. They had gathered in a square opposite the hospital. The National Bank, where Dziadek had worked since Mama's infancy, is right there. The protesters didn't march, but hovered, emitting heat and sound like gridlocked traffic. We had to get to the other side of the demonstration, but people wouldn't part for us like cars do for an ambulance. Dziadek pushed through them, repeating "*Przepraszam,*" moving students from side to side with his large, swollen-knuckled hands. I followed, bowing with apology. A freckled boy, not much older than my cousins, jumped back as if he'd just trampled me; a chubby man, his dirty hands wrapped around the pole of a flag, flinched as if I were a spider; and a girl with long black hair and a backpack slung over one shoulder smiled approvingly. Dziadek and I zigzagged through the crowd, the drone of people chanting around us, the hum of people talking near us, the vibrations of city traffic and streetcars beneath us, and suddenly the crowd parted and began to disperse, as if tired of Dziadek's insistent pushing. But it wasn't Dziadek's doing. There was a metal, mechanical sound similar to someone dragging chains across cobblestone, and the screeching of tires and car doors slamming. People started to run. I could see the pretty girl's backpack bobbing up and down in front of me as we neared the hospital. The fat man's belly was turning left and right and left again; he swivelled, unsure of whom to follow. The gap widened between Dziadek and me. He was trotting forward but his head snapped back towards me; he was shouting something. I could see a grey trunk rising above me some distance away, the sound of dragging chains getting closer. But it wasn't an elephant. And then my eyes stung, they stung and burned and filled with water. In a moment my face was completely wet. Dziadek turned to gather me up and I forced my face into the hollow of his collarbone, my eyes on fire. Even at six, I was a big child; I took up all of Dziadek. He squeezed me, hurting me as he lumbered on through the scattering crowd, there was whooshing and popping, and there was the pretty girl again, holding onto a woman, her teacher, a woman with a Solidarność poster who looked a lot like my mama. A woman who was my mama. My mama at the centre of a demonstration.

Inside the hospital, there was nearly as much noise as outside. I was pushed and pulled, left and right and left again. Someone held my head and splashed cold water on my face. They tilted my forehead and sprayed cold water into my eyes. Wet all over, eyelids refusing to part. When they tried to peel them open, I moaned.

I woke in the waiting room, my dizzy head in my mama's warm lap. Blurred figures on gurneys lined the hallway. My eyes, which had fallen deep into my head, retreating like scared animals into their subterranean shelters, still stung. Mama kissed me on each eye, her lips lingering on the lids, and I fell asleep again.

Only Mama and Dziadek got to see Babcia that day. Kids are too dirty and full of germs to visit patients with sick hearts. But the nurses should have looked at our sins, not our ages, to decide who was the filthiest of us all. "Thank God it happened before the demonstrators gathered," Dziadek said, looking at Mama, "otherwise she might have died in a gridlocked ambulance."

When Babcia came home a couple of days later, with pills to

take daily, she refused them, giving her and Dziadek one more thing to fight about. Dziadek would say, "I can't believe you're being so cavalier with your life," and she'd answer, "There are enough hypochondriacs like you around," or "So only *you* can be cavalier with my life." Then he would place one tiny pill in the middle of his palm and wait in front of her until she took it, with a huff. Sometimes when I stubbornly refuse to vacuum, or to get something from the store, and Babcia asks, "How did you get so petulant?" I say, "By watching you." She swats at me playfully like she's going to slap me in the head, I duck and we giggle.

I wake up from my crazy swimming dream on Dziadek's sofa, because Dziadek is taking plates out of the living room credenza and throwing them against the hardwood floor as if that's what they're made for. He doesn't see me: he is in combat mode. He has that same look on his face as he did the time he beat Kasia with his belt for playing with his diabetes pills as if they were marbles, the look that makes my stomach drop right onto my feet as if I've been cored, an apple to the baking pan. Where is Kasia? As the plates come crashing down, I realize they're ammunition. He throws the plates rhythmically: one *pow* two *boom* three *crash*! They smash and scatter into the four corners of the room, pieces rolling under the couch, some bouncing under the credenza, some even finding their way under the rug. Kasia is squatting under the table, hands flat on the rug, face barely visible behind the overhanging tablecloth.

Babcia should be attached to Dziadek's frenzied arm, shouting at him to stop, wrestling out of her husband's grasp the plates that her father the butcher painted with his own hands, setting them gently back in the credenza, but, instead she is laughing hysterically, as if Dziadek were wearing a red ball nose and rainbow-coloured hair and she watching this madness unfold under a circus tent. Standing in the doorway, I clench and unclench my fists to keep blood flowing.

Babcia's right cheekbone is purple and black, her face a rotten potato. She laughs so hard she rolls right off the couch, her feet hanging onto her high-heeled shoes only by the tips of her toes. "You're a bloody fool," she says to Dziadek, and throws her head back, hitting the carpet with a thud. She laughs again.

Dziadek is shaking, his red face quivering. He doesn't see me, but Kasia does. "If you touch a drop of alcohol again," he says to Babcia, "I swear to God, I will kill you."

"God?" Babcia exclaims. "God doesn't listen to two-faced comrades like you."

The pope and the Black Madonna look down from the wall at Babcia, sprawled on the carpet. Dziadek stands over her, a plate in his hand. "Kill me if you want," she says, "break my father's plates. Hit me. Leave me. I don't give a fuck."

"You've already done enough damage," Dziadek says and gestures at Babcia's face with the plate. "Look at you."

"How do you know I'm the one who did this?" Babcia closes her eyes. For a second she looks still and colourless, fast asleep, almost dead. "Pathetic," she says quietly. "Absolutely pathetic."

I don't know if she's talking about herself, Dziadek, or perhaps all of us.

Dziadek sets the last of the blue and white plates back in the now nearly empty cabinet. What remains is a full set of dessert plates, teacups and saucers. But you can't subsist on dessert alone, as Babcia says at Sunday dinners when I go straight for the sweets instead of the meat and potatoes.

FIVE

ON AN UNCHARACTERISTICALLY HOT, early September morning, the ringing phone wakes me. My heart, expertly trained for emergencies and still a bit jittery from the start of the new school year, is thumping in my throat. Since I had already kicked the covers off in the middle of the night, catapulting myself out of the bottom bunk is easy.

Babcia is talking on the phone in the living room, groggy and mad. I eavesdrop from the hallway, swaying a little, chewing on my fingernails.

"I can't continue like this. It's been over two years. I'm an old woman." Her voice is shallow, muffled, like someone's holding her under water.

Babcia *is* old. On Christmas Day, when we will celebrate another great martyr in addition to her, Babcia will turn sixty. She'll plop a live carp into the bathtub and tell Kasia and me to watch it in order to distract us from the fact that we should be drawing birthday cards for her. When we dare sing *Sto Lat,* the happy birthday song, she will wave her hands as if to disperse mosquitoes and say, "A hundred years? Bah! I'll be lucky if I make it to sixty-five," and she will disappear into the steaming kitchen like a priest into a cloud of frankincense at midnight Mass.

I push the living room door a millimetre and bring my eye

to the opening. Babcia is sitting on the edge of the sofa, wearing a nightgown that appears voluminous due to the draft from the open window. A hairnet holds her hair in place. Fat down pillows lie misshapen, ditto the duvet. Babcia sleeps under thousands of feathers even in the most suffocating of summers. "It's good to sweat a little," she says. And that's why she gives me scorching tea with lemon and sugar when it's hot out and I'm thirsty, except when it's a special occasion and people come to the house. Then there's dried fruit *kompot* in the fridge.

I sit on the hallway rug where Mama and Tata fought almost-to-the-death the day before Kasia was born. I sit cross-legged, a flexible yogi. Mama did yoga a few times at the community centre in Morena and said it 'opened her up.' Being opened up doesn't sound appealing to me.

Babcia is too calm for this to be an emergency phone call. It must be Mama, which would make this a rare and costly calm, a long-overdue, long-distance calm. Babcia is holding the receiver with both hands, like it weighs more than anything she's ever held before. "It's not about money," she says. "There is money. Don't send money."

We get plastic things that Tata brings home from Asia once a year and meat that Babcia sneaks home from her supermarket-supplier job, but is there really money? And should she be saying these things into the telephone held with both hands, speaking so clearly, her words for everyone to hear? Maybe it's too early for the operator and the authorities to be awake. Or maybe Dziadek's bank connections got us the only untapped line.

Babcia doesn't say anything for a long time, just fingers her forehead and squeezes it, making it wrinkle and un-wrinkle like the accordion her crazy brother, Wujek Kamil, plays at baptisms and weddings. Every few seconds she lets out a noise, which I know is meant to sound like an agreeable 'mhm' but is instead a small animal-like moan. Finally, in a surprisingly alert and direct tone, she says, "You just have to make a decision, Ewa, either way. Pick one and do it. No more dawdling and sitting on your hands."

What is she saying? I'm always on Babcia's side, except right now. Don't give Mama a choice. Tell her to come home. Now. I clench my fists so hard I swear my nails are puncturing my skin. I don't get a choice. There is a lump in my throat the size of a shot put. I wish I had a shot put right now to bust through the window and make a spectacle. If Mama doesn't come home I will stop doing homework and fail all my tests. I will run all the way to Gdynia and break all my useless joints once and for all. They will have to push me around in a rusty wheelchair.

Mama is now audible through the phone, but she isn't yelling or cursing. She is slow and loud, explaining, defensive. The wind whines, drafts push into the hallway, opening the living room door three millimetres more.

"You're going to kill me, Ewa. You're going to kill me and I'll be dead and then who'll take care of the girls?" Babcia lifts her head slowly, notices me sitting on the carpet. I smile. It must be a sad-clown sort of smile, but I can't think of what else to do. I don't want Mama to kill Babcia, or anyone else or anything else to kill Babcia. I keep smiling like a buffoon while considering what to do. I make Babcia smile, too. She mirrors what I do, that's why her smile is as taut as an elastic band in a slingshot, a smile absurd next to her hooded eyes.

Babcia makes an upward gesture with her chin at me and says into the phone, "Gosia is going to say hello."

I lumber into the living room and sit down heavily on the couch beside Babcia. I lay my head against her chest. She holds onto me.

"Hi," I say into the receiver.

Mama says, "Good morning, my lovely. Did I wake you? It won't be long. I'm working on it. It won't be long."

When we hang up I make the collar of Babcia's nightgown

72

all wet and she kisses my head many times and rubs my shoulder softly.

IT'S BEEN A COUPLE of weeks and Mama has called every single day. She spends all her money on long-distance phone calls instead of sending it here, and she and Babcia bicker like they did over my first communion dress. I'm allowed to say a quick hello after each fight. Mama makes her voice all high and slow for me, and sometimes I can tell she is breathing in the middle of sentences to prevent herself from crying. She says, "I'll see you soon. I promise." Dziadek tries to grab the phone out of Babcia's or my hand, but we win, because there are two of us.

I AM FINALLY GETTING some good grades, although mainly because of the excitement and happiness I feel about Mama finally coming home. No one's actually said, "Mama's coming home," but I can feel it. I'm so happy I study all the time. Even my reading has gotten better. I've memorized the stupid Cyrillic alphabet, which nobody in my class has been able to do. When Babcia saw my first Russian test with the perfect mark on it, she told me I've got the makings of a real Communist. "You're definitely your Dziadek's granddaughter." When Dziadek saw it, he said, "Certainly it's your Babcia's Bolshevik blood." But I don't actually speak Russian. I just write the letters, intricate curls, like the doodles in my notebook. My Russian teacher says I'm a natural, which makes me embarrassed because it is *Russian* after all, and my classmates say "of course you're good at it, you are a *Ruski*," except Beata Kowalska, who understands how nice it is to finally be good at something, no matter what it is, and to get positive attention.

IT'S THE LAST weekend of September and Dziadek's annual name-day celebration, a two-day event—one dinner with family, the other with officials from the bank. Babcia is not the only one who pretends her birthday doesn't exist; Dziadek says birthdays are for children who are still counting up, whereas old people who are counting down celebrate their patron saint instead of the day of their birth. The Feast Day. We will feast indeed, until we feel like puking.

Tomorrow, the whole family is coming to Oliwa for a dinner of tripe and jellied and pickled things. Mama's siblings, our cousins, Babcia's sister Ciocia Fela, even crazy Wujek Kamil, will shower the clan leader, our Dziadek (who was named after the Archangel Michał) with bonbons, vodka and flowers. I can't help but hear Mama say, "Some angel," sucking air into her cheeks through clenched teeth.

The kitchen has been taken over by Babcia, who is cooking with both bought and smuggled ingredients. Thirsty or hungry, we are under strict orders to keep out, or we might risk losing a finger under a parsley- or onion-chopping cleaver, or skin a hand on a horseradish- or carrot-mincing box grater.

Even though it's drizzling out, Kasia is downstairs in the sandbox building muddy pies with her friends. When I ask Dziadek if I can go, too, he says, "You're too big."

"Plus Babcia needs you to set the table," he says.

"But dinner's tomorrow night," I say. "It's only Friday."

Tonight we will have a simple, meatless dinner—like every Friday—of scrambled eggs, cod or fried eel. We will watch the news on channel one and then an old movie on channel two. If it's a Rita Hayworth movie, Babcia will be in a good mood and we'll get dessert, even though we're not supposed to on Fridays. Babcia doesn't know Rita Hayworth was Jewish, but I do, because Beata Kowalska told me. I haven't told Babcia because I like when she's in a good mood.

"Just set the table," Dziadek says.

Babcia never asks me to set the table. She does it herself. "Why can't you do it?" I say.

Now it's Dziadek who's frowning. We bicker. I pose arguments for why I deserve to be outside in the wet playground instead of inside doing chores. I outline how good I've been. "I have a five in Russian," I moan. "The best mark."

"I thought they did sixes now."

"Next year," I say, and stick my tongue out a little once he turns around.

Dziadek goes for the credenza, unlocks a top cupboard, while I squirm and shrink into myself, expecting plates to smash and ricochet against the floor. Instead of plates, he drops a wad of letters on the table.

"Here," he says. "Open them."

I've seen Mama's letters before. "So?" I say, and shrug.

"Read them."

Dziadek has a weird look on his face, like he's trying to convince me to jump out of a plane without a parachute. Like it's war and it's got to be me or him, and he'd rather it be me.

"What do I need to read them for?"

"There're things in them you should know," Dziadek says calmly. He sits at the table, places both hands on the lace tablecloth, his fingers badly misshapen from arthritis.

I sit across from him, and here we are, two comrades ready to negotiate.

"Can you just tell me?"

If he still smoked, he'd be smoking right now. That's what people do when they're frazzled. The sharp scent of horseradish wafts from the kitchen, the rhythmic grating, like the sound of twigs cracking underfoot in an autumn forest. Babcia, who's barricaded herself, is probably hunched over a large plastic bowl at the sink with the window wide open, crying over the gnarled, spicy root. No matter how many tears she sheds, no matter how many fingers she skins or how puffy her eyes get, Babcia refuses to get store-bought horseradish. We're not having an ordinary Friday dinner, just the four of us.

"Who's coming for dinner?" I ask.

Dziadek looks at me. He's sort of impressed that I've figured it out. "Your mother is ready for you to come to Canada," he says.

"To visit, for winter vacation," I clarify, "for Christmas?"

Dziadek shakes his head absentmindedly.

"I don't get it."

"Now," he says. "You'll go now."

Now? But school has started. There is no holiday now. We just had summer holidays a month ago. What about school? Who is going to do my work for me? How will I catch up? But I can't ask these questions because all I can think is that I finally get to see Mama. After twenty-eight months, I get to touch and see and smell and be with my mama.

Before Dziadek can say anything else, I'm jumping up and down like I weigh fifty kilos again, my hands looped around his neck, jumping and kissing my grandfather. I've got quite the chokehold on him. He takes my hands. "So you're excited?" Dziadek smiles.

The only time I've been outside of Poland was when Mama took me to Denmark with her to visit a friend from university. Canada is a great distance away, and we don't have that much time. We can't miss too much school or else we'll have to repeat, like stupid Piotrek. We'll have to take a plane.

Babcia and Dziadek have decided to share this best-news-ever with Tata. They've invited him for dinner. When was the last time they talked? It was so long ago that I have no recollection of all of them being in the same room. Nevertheless, it was before "Tata's treachery," before his walking out on Mama and "all of his paternal responsibilities," as Dziadek often likes to sum up. We won't be having scrambled eggs, cod or fried eel; we'll have carp, like on Christmas Eve, because Babcia is trying to impress Tata with something special, and in our family, a bottom-dwelling shit-eating lake fish is special.

In anticipation of Tata's arrival at the puny Oliwa apartment (he will look like Gulliver in Lilliput here), I hide in the bathroom and keep our dinner company. The carp is the slimiest and the fattest one we've ever had. The fish rolls gently, knocking its fleshy lips into the porcelain, completing two body lengths of the bathtub before having to turn around and swim back the other way. His slippery pucker, a feeble kiss on my skin. My hand blocks his path.

This September-Christmas carp is more of a porpoise than a fish. He's big, but harmless. The only aggressive thing about him is his sharp, pleated fin that juts out of the water. I feel sorry for him; he's so awkward in the tub, somewhat panicked, gulping for air. He must know what's coming—Babcia's cleaver—because he thrashes like no other carp I've tended to before. I open the faucet to let in more cold water, the stream disorienting the fish.

"Don't bother," I hear Babcia shout from the kitchen, "he'll be dead in two minutes."

Tata will be here soon. Kasia and I are freshly clothed. Dziadek is fumbling with shoe polish. The table is pushed up to the couch for extra seating and set with one extra place, as per Christmas Eve ritual, for a wandering traveller. This is weird. Why is Babcia recreating Christmas Eve? I thought she was just showing off her connections, proving we don't go hungry—albeit my size is proof enough. No rations here. She has also decorated, which is rare. There are chrysanthemums in Babcia's prized crystal vase and paper napkins under slightly tarnished silver cutlery. I wonder if she will leave out a winter boot on the windowsill and fill it with chocolates and clementines, a present for Tata from Saint Nicholas.

A thin stream trickles into the tub and I ladle water onto the fish's back with both hands. The carp's almost entirely submerged when I notice that my white blouse is wet all down the front where my boobs were tightly pressed against the side of the tub.

Kasia slips into the bathroom. "What are you doing?" she whispers.

"Watch where you're going," I say, but it's too late. Her brown tights are already darker at the toes where she's stepped into the puddle.

"Aw, it's wet," she whines. She sits beside me. "Move. Let's see."

"He's suffocating," I say, continuing to splash the fish.

"But Babcia said not to waste water."

She reaches and unscrews a bottle of Babcia's sage shampoo, and before I can inflict pain on her, she drizzles a ribbon of the dark green liquid into the stream pouring out of the faucet. Iridescent foam grows; the carp's fin now bisects a path of bubbles. Dziadek opens the door and we duck, instinctively. He narrows his eyes, more stressed than mad. He fixes on my contorted body, legs splayed, bum flattened, about as graceful as a walrus. Now he looks mad.

"Get up!" Dziadek barks. "Get up right now."

We do as he says, wet and wrinkled, dishevelled like we're two and three, not six and eleven.

"Look at you," he says, bits of spit shooting out of his mouth. "You'd be more respectful if you were the ones who had to do the laundry and the ironing. Or if your mother did."

When he leaves I close my fist and punch Kasia in the arm as hard as I can. "Holy shit!" she yelps, teeters, and nearly falls into the bubble bath. She whimpers, fat tears forming fast. "I hate you," she cries, "lard ass." We rinse the confused carp with fresh water before delivering him to Babcia for slaughter.

I was right. In Babcia and Dziadek's apartment Tata looks like an obese man in a little kid's jacket. As soon as he walks through the front door, he absorbs the narrow hallway completely, a train in a tunnel. All the rest of us can do is walk backwards to get out of the way. He looks bigger than in the parking lot, larger than at the beach, wider than in his car. It's as if the ceiling here is lower than any place else, because Tata slouches as he walks. He has the power to shrink our surroundings with one forceful knock on the door.

He's wearing a sweater the colour of a sheep, with a white shirt collar peeking out at the top. He hands Babcia a bunch of red carnations, which Mama always called 'Communist funeral flowers.' Babcia hates them, too, but she thanks Tata nonetheless. His goatee is longer than when we were at the beach, and the moustache part is a little coiled, like Cardinal Richelieu's from The Musketeers. His face scratches mine as he kisses each cheek, holding me by the shoulders. His sweater is scratchy and damp, way too warm for this weather. Despite Tata's remoteness, I feel confined and winded, and suddenly feel devastatingly sad for the slimy fish. Kasia gets a hug, but she doesn't wrap her arms around him this time. She's limp, obedient. Once Tata is seated on the living room sofa, he seems smaller and there is more air for everyone else to breathe. I sit, too, and exhale, my chest sinking toward my belly.

The grown-ups swap niceties about weather and appearances: oh what a mild fall, finally rain for harvest, rain after such a hot summer, Dziadek is keeping well, Babcia seems healthy, Tata's sweater is smart. But once the recently killed and fried carp is served, and boiled potatoes with skins on them, and Russian salad of boiled vegetables, apples, eggs, pickles and mayonnaise, there is fuel for the real reason Tata is here.

"Ewa is a rich Canadian now," Tata says out of the blue. "So I think there's no more need for child support."

We watch Tata eat, devouring the first meal Babcia has prepared for him in years. "You won't need my money when you're in Canada." Tata turns to me. My face is on fire. "I'm not going to pay for things if she takes you away."

Even though Kasia hates me, she is burrowing herself into my soft flesh. Her bird-like frame fits wholly under my arm.

"Why don't you eat, *córeczko*," Tata says to Kasia. He never calls me *córeczko*: too diminutive and delicate for Małgorzata. I wonder whether he'll choke on the bones in the fish for using a word that doesn't belong to him, for using Babcia's word.

"I know she has somebody there," Tata says to Dziadek and Babcia, who sit on the opposite side of the table from him, Solidarność union representatives in front of a general. Tata is solid and stiff, immovable. "She does, doesn't she?" he presses. His question hovers for a second above the table.

Yes! I want to shout to make him stop staring crazily at Babcia and Dziadek. She has her students, and some dog.

"Ewa needs your consent to take the children out of the country," Dziadek says. "Without your permission the girls cannot visit their mother." Dziadek sits in front of his food with his hands folded on his lap, his grey jacket matching grey pants meant to be worn for official business, meetings and parades. Mama called this colour gunmetal grey. Dziadek doesn't dress like this for just anyone. "You wouldn't want to be responsible for keeping mother and children apart any longer."

Tata ignores Dziadek. "I asked you a question," he growls and looks right at me, canine eyes illuminated by the overhead light fixture.

I point at my chest. Me? How am I the best person in the room to confirm if Mama has *someone* in Canada? She is too busy working, preparing for lessons and saving money; she has no time for socializing. Plus she didn't go there to meet someone; she has plenty of someones here. Kasia twitches, jamming her skinny elbow into my rib.

"Leave the girl alone," Babcia snaps.

"Shhh," Dziadek grumbles. "Don't interfere."

Babcia stands, lifts the platter and releases a piece of the greasy fish onto Tata's plate. It lands with a slap. Tata doesn't flinch; instead, he holds my gaze. His eyes glow. They're a strange colour, *piwne*, the colour of beer and amber. "Dog piss and pine shit," Babcia would say. She prefers cognac and doesn't wear jewellery. "Jewels are for Russian whores who cover up their sins with silver fox fur."

Outside, the rain has picked up, a downpour now. I want to answer Tata's question, but words are stuck behind my sealed lips. I can hear Mama say, 'Tell him to pick on people his own size. If he has questions about my private life tell him to call me and ask me himself.' Veins bulge in Tata's muscular forearms. I look down at my hands. "I don't know," I whisper.

"Do you want to go to Canada?"

"I—" I begin, stuttering like Piotrek Kwiatkowski. My mouth is open, tracing the words, but no sound. Mute like a carp. I close my eyes to finish the sentence. "I don't know."

"You think you'll like Canada better than your homeland?" Tata says. "Do you?" He thrusts his head closer to mine. I take short breaths to avoid inhaling his musty smell. "You think you'll be happier with your mother and her gigolo?"

I don't know what gigolo means. Who is the gigolo? It must be Mama's *he*, the same person Tata invents for his bullying and manipulation. Whoever or whatever the gigolo is, I suddenly regret being so stubborn and refusing to read Mama's grown-up letters. People do a lot of talking in code around me. I never cared much to decipher that code, but now that sweat is collecting in the crease in my belly and in the divot above my lip, I wish I had paid more attention, invested more effort.

"That's enough," Dziadek says. Now he is standing, but not to offer Tata food. I tear skin from around my thumbnail. A sickle of blood forms. I put the thumb in my mouth. The taste of coins.

"You're going to suck your thumb?" Tata barks. "Instead of talking to your father you're going to suck your thumb, like a little kid?"

Kasia frees herself from under my arm, suddenly alert. She props herself on the edge of the couch with hyper-extended arms, chin barely clearing the table. "I'm a little kid," she says, "and I don't suck my thumb."

Dziadek sits and Tata eats the rest of the lukewarm carp. He taps his knife and fork loudly. The chrysanthemums are fiery under the light of the ugly chandelier.

TATA LEAVES BEFORE dessert of *makowiec* and *kompot*. We put the sweets away for tomorrow and clean up; even Dziadek joins the assembly line of scraping, washing, drying and putting away. It all flows smoothly and silently. It's crowded in the kitchen with Dziadek there.

The rainstorm sounds like herring thrown down from heaven, the fish slapping with great force against the windowpanes and windowsills. When the dishes, pots and cutlery are all in their proper places, Dziadek says, "Let's have a drink." We look at him the way people look at me when I walk down the street holding Babcia's hand. "Extenuating circumstances," Dziadek says, though none of us has said anything. Babcia grins slyly. You're not supposed to have alcohol on Friday.

"To Canada," he says, and raises a stubby glass.

"To our vacation with Mama," I add. Kasia beams.

We sit in the living room and watch the rain beat up the tiny balcony. Raindrops bounce so high off the railing that it could be raining from the bottom up. No gravity. No gravity would be nice. Dziadek doesn't mind that Babcia is having more cognac. It's after midnight, and Babcia starts singing *Sto Lat* to Dziadek whose name day it is. Dziadek joins her in another drink and a song. He's singing in honour of himself. Even Kasia and I have sips of celebratory booze. The sips set my insides on fire, an all-over-body, bubble bath feeling. When we're all good and calm, tickled in throats and bellies with cognac, we go to sleep on the living room sofa, squished together as if we have no other options, as if we won't see each other for a very long time.

PART II

ZERO

PEOPLE TELL STORIES. They can't help themselves. Predictable stories, repetitive stories, stories only they know and only they can tell. "Therefore," Dziadek announced after completing another World War II story, "all stories are true," except when he would tell us how he ended up in the concentration camp Stutthof. He didn't follow it up with "true story," because he'd never finish that story.

Dziadek's signature stories are about the war; Babcia's are about God and the church; Mama's are political. Tata only ever told one story that I remember. This is because he told it as often as he took us to the Oliwa Zoo, which was too often. During the uphill hike from the wild cats area to the American buffalo enclosure he would launch into the story about his big decathlon, about the time of anticipation and disappointment, the time between completing day one and beginning day two of the contest.

Tata said that with five gruelling events completed, decathletes take a well deserved rest before it is time to get up and do it all over again the next morning, this time on tired legs, with gummy arms, an anxious mind and some experience behind them. They had run in a dash, crossed land in a leap, moved iron in a toss, got light-headed in a jump and succeeded in an endurance sprint. For some decathletes, rest came in the form of a warm, salty bath, for others, a doughy, rolling massage. Tata said he always chose to eat a meal with friends. Some of his teammates ate alone in front of a television. In whatever form rest came, for several hours decathletes' bodies were still.

Although tranquil and still, they were not extinguished. They readied for the second half of the endurance test, humbled by day one's results, looking forward to new tests, full of altered hope. Attitudes were shifted by the quality and quantity of the evening's rest.

"Here's exactly what happened in my final year," Tata told us, "when I was competing in Poznań. Part of the stadium burned down, overnight, poof, up in flames while we all slept. So they moved us to smaller venues all over the city, which was incredibly tedious. But that's how I met your mother."

Mama worked as a translator for the Ministry of Sport, a summer job that paid her more in connections for a future teaching job than it did in *złoty*. It was her responsibility to explain to Tata's Swedish roommate that he was supposed to be at the city track not the university track for his next event. "Thanks to your mother the guy made it to the right place in the nick of time," Tata told me. "It was the first time in years a Soviet didn't take the whole thing." He paused. "I did the best I'd ever done."

IT HAD BEEN a couple of weeks since Tata's fake Christmas dinner, when Dziadek suddenly delivered our airline tickets with his sober bureaucrat face. Our Canadian visit was happening—now—regardless of anything else. I had no idea what to expect, just Mama's thin face, which in my mind was beginning to fade like an old newspaper clipping. In Kasia's suitcase Babcia packed dried mushrooms, jams, tablecloths, slippers, doilies and other random gifts she thought Mama would need. Mama only needs us, I thought as I sorted through piles of starched and ironed clothes. Our neighbour, Beata Kowalska, came into our room while I was packing. Beata said, "You're lucky you get to go to Canada." She sat on the floor, her stick legs stretched out. "My tata's been all over the place, but Mama and I haven't been anywhere."

"Ours too," I said, and nodded. I threw my Lechia Gdańsk t-shirt into the suitcase, even though it's grotesquely too small. Piotrek Kwiatkowski calls it my 'titty top.'

"Your mother's been to places," Beata said, "and you went to Denmark with her."

"But you guys go on vacation, to Bulgaria *and* Romania, all the time." *And* Beata's parents are at home when they aren't working. Together. At home in Morena with their only daughter who gets all their attention. Beata's last name, Kowalska, comes from the word blacksmith. Suddenly, I pictured marvellous heavy horseshoes attached to the bottoms of her skinny feet and felt incredibly envious of how rooted she is here. No one can move her from this place, despite her slight built. And I got so jealous.

"Those aren't places," Beata said. She picked up my Barbie, who lay on a stack of shirts and pants, and twirled her, sticking Barbie's pointed feet into her hands and rubbing them together. The doll's hair flailed about ridiculously.

"Of course they are places." I snatched Barbie from Beata's hands. "All places are places."

"They're *Russian* places," Beata sneered. "They're not *real* places like Canada or Denmark or England." Beata was flipping my Europe cassette in her hand. "Can I have this?"

"No!"

Beata looked at me in the same way I look at Kasia when she throws her tantrums. "Jesus," she said, "you can get yourself fifty more in Canada."

"This was a present from my mama," I said.

"You can be so selfish, you know."

Beata's insult hovered in mid-air, a hungry seagull. I sat on the floor with my legs splayed, torso slumped over knees, sandwiching the cassette in my palms like a prayer book. I'm not selfish, I thought. I'm protective.

"Here," I said, thrusting the tape into Beata's altar-flat chest. "Have it."

Her eyebrows went first one up and one down, slumping sadly over her ordinary blue eyes. "No, man." She pushed my hand away. "I was kidding." She giggled nervously. "It was a present from your mama. Just leave me your posters."

"How long do you think I'm going to be gone?" Now I was the one laughing stupidly. "George, Sting and Joey are staying exactly where they are."

Instead of giving away my creased posters from smuggled German magazines, I let Beata listen to 'The Final Countdown' not once but three times in a row. We danced, arms flailing over our heads, torsos jerking up and down, our canvas runners lifting off the carpet during the chorus.

THE FIRST THING I notice about Canada is that dogs here don't bark. A stewardess escorts us to the luggage area, where people stand with their polite dogs. "Watch for your bags coming around the corner," Pani Alicja says, and points to the conveyor belt.

Kasia and I nod.

Dziadek has lent me a hardback suitcase with metal clasps. The bag Kasia has is on loan from Ciocia Fela, a navy blue sack on wheels that extends like a fire truck ladder when vertical compartments are unzipped.

"You have to pull with all your might," Pani Alicja says. "I'd stay and help you, but I've got to run." She kisses the air around our cheeks and squeezes Kasia's shoulders. "And over there—" She points to glass doors separating the luggage area from masses of people—"is where your mother will be."

We scan for Mama and don't notice Pani Alicja's outstretched hand tugging the Unaccompanied Minor sign that hangs around Kasia's neck. "I have to take this back," she says. Thankfully, she doesn't ask for mine. At some point between hours four and five of the flight, after my third Coke and before the first of my three 7Ups, while most passengers were fast asleep (Kasia snoring like Babcia), I tucked my Unaccompanied Minor sign into my carry-on, which is really my school backpack. I made sure no one was watching. It fit perfectly between my notebook and a fat envelope of documents Dziadek made me swear on Babcia's grave I wouldn't lose. No more stupid label on my chest.

During hour two of the flight, as I waddled to the teeny washroom at the very end of the long narrow aisle, hips grazing every seat and elbows tucked in to avoid collisions, every passenger I passed stared at the plastic sign obstructing my overdeveloped chest. "Unaccompanied *minor*?" each of them seemed to say. I could see the question marks, the judgement, in their narrowed eyes. "There is nothing minor about *her.*" And the fine print on my boobs: Destination Toronto, Ewa Wasiljewska. I am a parcel sent across the Atlantic to Mama. Airmail. Oversize. So big I should really be sent via cargo ship, take months instead of hours to get there. I'm Gulliver in Lilliput.

As soon as Kasia hands over the sign, Pani Alicja sprints away. She waves goodbye and her slender form disappears into crowds moving in the opposite direction.

The Mama I am expecting is slender. She has long brown hair that's soft to the touch—too soft, she always said—flyaway hair. It falls on her shoulders and curls up at the ends. Can't stay put. She has grey eyes that look almost silver in the light, like seagull wing tips. Her limbs are long and sinewy. She would look nice in a stewardess uniform. The nails on her long fingers are painted red when she's happy, red like the poppies on the fringes of Babcia's garden.

"PAY ATTENTION," Kasia hisses. "We don't want someone to steal our bags."

"They're way too big to steal."

"Whatever," she says. "Pay attention."

When Kasia and I wrestle our suitcases off the luggage carousel and drag them through the doors, my heart is beating so hard I can hardly concentrate. Kasia says, "Where are we going now?"

"To church, and then for ice cream."

Kasia makes a face. "You know, Babcia says sarcasm is the laziest form of humour."

"No she doesn't," I say, and pull away.

At the mention of Babcia, my eyes get hot and my lips shrink into a tiny, sad line, like a snail that's been poked with a cruel kid finger. I might start bawling. Kasia shuffles behind. When we get to a clearing in the terminal, I lean my bag by a column and Kasia perches her butt on it. "And now what?" she demands.

"And now we wait," I say.

BABCIA AND DZIADEK couldn't go past security with us at the airport in Warszawa. Babcia kissed the worried look on my face and said, "It's been a long time coming. Just enjoy this." But Kasia and I cried. Babcia cried too, like an old woman, mostly with her eyes, whereas Kasia's whole body moved up and down like a jackhammer and there was a rope of snot between her lip and her nostril. I got a headache from all the crying and my eyes went puffy like the Canadian bubble envelopes Mama sends Smurf pyjamas and pompom socks in. Dziadek stood on the periphery of the wet goodbyes, his hands folded across his middle, the way they are when he watches Mass.

Babcia said, "Write to me as soon as you get there," and snot ran into the divot above her lip. "Or draw me something." At least Babcia knows me. She wiped the snot and tears away with her sleeve. "I'll pray to *Matka Boska* and *Ojciec Święty* that you get there safely."

We covered one another with our arms and shoulders. Even Dziadek embraced us for longer than one second and kissed us on the cheeks instead of the eye or the forehead. "Give a kiss to your mother for me."

Babcia handed us two paper bags with food. I shoved mine inside the suitcase so I wouldn't have to hold it. The paper was dry, like Babcia's hand, which I wanted to be holding. Now Kasia says, "Something smells really bad." The smell is subtle, yet persistent, like a fart. I open the bag and pull out the package Babcia prepared for me. Now the smell is much more potent. The contents of the brown bag are sweaty and pungent: a greenish hard-boiled egg, a tomato that used to be whole, a pouch made of newspaper that holds a mixture of salt and pepper, a ham sandwich made with lots of bread, a slice of ham and a few slices of wet pickle and stinky kiełbasa.

"Fuck," I curse, "what a waste," and toss the food into a nearby trashcan. I miss, and everything scatters over the shiny floor.

"I ate mine," Kasia says.

"Good for you, fatso."

There where the mangled tomato has rolled stands Mama, a woman who looks nothing like our mama but is in fact our mama. She looks like one of my shorn, fake Barbies. Everything—including my heart—stops when I see her. This is what I imagine being dead feels like. Complete stillness, yet all the cells in your body—especially in the eyes, face and chest—feel like they're going to burst.

Mama just stands there, too, but only for a moment. She must be shocked at how gigantic I am. It's definitely her, even though her hair is wrong. It's Mama's big, perfect smile, teeth whiter than her skin, whiter than her unpainted nails, whiter than the whites of her eyes. Those are her childish dimples. But her hair is almost as white as her teeth; colourless blonde, and short like a boy's.

She runs toward us, like people at airports do in the movies, and wraps herself around us. I inhale all of her, clean and sweet like fresh linen, but not like my mama. She doesn't have that familiar smoke smell I remember.

"Finally," she says, over and over. "Finally."

Her dimples, her lips, new wrinkles coming from her eyes like rays in my cartoon sun drawings. Her boy-hair, her long neck, the summer-brown freckles across her nose. "Too busy to do long hair," she says, and she kisses the surprised look on my face. It's so strange to be nearly level with my mama's kiss, not to have her come down to me like an eyelash-fluttering giraffe at the Oliwa Zoo.

A skinny man hovers behind her, so skinny, in fact, that I don't notice him during the kissing and embracing. He wears glasses that take up most of his face, and a grimace that he wouldn't be able to curl into a smile even if he tried really hard.

"This is my good friend, Pan Rousseau," Mama says, and pushes the skinny man toward us. He's a shy first communion recipient and I'm a priest. "You can't trust short men," Tata used to say. "Short men always have something to prove." Pan Rousseau has greying hair that's too long for an old man, and looks more like a mad professor than a good friend. He's got a thin patchy beard, but no moustache, which is really weird and looks like a glued-on disguise. Maybe he doesn't want to be seen with us? Mama shifts from one foot to the other. She wears sneakers, meant for exercising, not for special occasions. She runs a thumbnail across her teeth. When she catches me watching her, she smiles, and puts her hand in the pocket of her jeans. I don't want to make Mama feel more nervous, so I glance at Kasia. Kasia kisses Mama's friend three times on the cheeks.

"Call me Serge," Pan Rousseau says in Polish, "mister makes me feel so old."

Mama shoots him a quick glance. "How about *Wujek* Serge?"

I refuse to call some stranger in disguise 'uncle,' even if he supposedly is Mama's friend. It's creepy. And Serge is the most crooked sounding, unfinished name. Maybe it's Russian—Sergei—and he's ashamed of it, so he shortened it. Serge sounds like a skidding car to me. Even his last name is abnormal—*rosół*, chicken soup—unlike my name, which is as ordinary as swastikas in stairwells. It's like all girls born in the mid-to-late seventies had to be named Beata, Agnieszka or Małgorzata, and all the boys Piotrek, Michał or Andrzej, so nobody would be special.

"My mother was Polish and my father's French-Canadian," Pan Rousseau says. The Polish he speaks is sweet and mushy, pudding in the mouth; he talks like a toddler. "I was born in Canada. My mother taught me her language."

Not very well.

"So your mother's dead?" Kasia says with the same sad face she sports while praying.

"She died of cancer when I was about your age," Pan Rousseau replies, looking at me. "Fifteen or so." I'm not even close to fifteen.

The egg and bread I attempted to chuck lie pathetically on the floor. I toss all of it in the trash; even after it's all gone, I still pick at the floor. Only when Mama puts her hand on my hunched back do I rise and wipe my hands on my sweatpants. If Pan Rousseau doesn't know that I'm eleven, I wonder what else he doesn't know about us, or Mama, or Gdańsk, or anything important for that matter.

As we walk out of the terminal I am a knock-kneed idiot. I nearly collide with a woman carrying a small child in her arms. She looks at me like I'm an invader from outer space. "Przepraszam," I mumble.

Mama is one step ahead of me. I try to match her stride but this only highlights how big and wide I am. She's a slender shadow of me. "I'm so happy to see you," she says, and gives me an awkward side hug once we're in step with one another. A peck on my cheek follows. "My gorgeous girl."

I pull away from Mama. She tries to take a hold of my hand, but I hide it in my pocket.

When we come to a stop at the sliding doors, she brings her face toward mine and rests her forehead on my shoulder so lightly that she's almost not there at all. I pat her on the back.

"You will always be my baby, no matter how tall you get or how much I shrink." I have no intention of growing any taller. She draws me closer to her again and kisses my forehead. Her lips are dry. She smacks them like she has no spit left, the opposite of my moist, slightly motion-sick mouth.

An impressively large black car pulls into the bay in front of us. It is fit for Chairman Jaruzelski and General Secretary Gorbachev to travel around in, except it's missing the red and white flags on its hood. We girls sit in the back, while Pan Rousseau talks to the driver, who wears an official-looking hat that sits high on his forehead. People in Poland don't talk to men who wear uniforms, especially hats, unless they are threatened. Mama sits in the middle, her skinny knees grazing her chest, her arms wide around us. Kasia burrows into Mama's torso, her arms encircling Mama's waist and reaching my side of the car. I hate her arms so close to me, on my side of Mama.

Mama leans into me and says, "You'll like where we live. I think you'll be happy here."

Happy? Here?

If I were alone right now, I'd be bawling so hard that I'd forget how to breathe. I'd be gulping for air like the fake-Christmas carp, and snot would be running over my lip. But because I can't do any of that, I shut my eyes tight until I'm not here at all. It's all black inside my head, deafening, and I'm flying once more.

Then Mama says, "Could we please drive a little faster?" and I am back.

Spit is collecting in my mouth faster than I can swallow, and I breathe, breathe hard into my soft belly to keep myself from puking, or crying, or both at once.

Mama says, "Could we please drive a little faster?" The chatter of the radio, the driver and Pan Rousseau, Kasia's manic giggles and her stories of the flight, the odd bump and swerve of the car underneath me and Mama stroking strands of my hair and tucking them behind my hot ear above me all add up to the fact that I am going crazy. I want to scream "STOP!" but it's all moving too fast for me to open my mouth. Suddenly I can't even remember how long Mama was gone for, or that she was gone at all, or that she's back and we are together and I am *here,* reclining on her lap, because all I can think of is Babcia. Where is Babcia and where am I in relation to *her?*

ON THE WAY to his house, Pan Rousseau asks the limo driver to stop at the grocery store. The chaos inside the car stops for a moment and I actually lift my sick head to see. The store is called Miracle and there are no lineups outside. Pan Rousseau buys strange things—ginger ale, a spicy soda he says will help my stomach, and mint ice cream, peanut butter and bread that can't hold anything up and has to be cooked to be used. The things he buys are odd, but, like Lego blocks, they come in beautiful, multicoloured boxes and plastic wrapping that doesn't have the chemical Made-in-Taiwan smell that I'm used to from the things Tata brings us.

In a place called North York, in a house on a street lined with low pale houses, with sad willow trees and old maples, Mama has prepared *gołąbki* for our arrival. "We will eat them with toast," she says, "and have ice cream afterwards." In Poland, mint is for stomach-soothing tea, not for dessert. After our bags are unloaded from the trunk of the car, after we enter this strange house in this strange neighbourhood and after our strange mama sits me down, I drink Pan Rousseau's ginger ale and the bubbles run right into my nose and out my mouth. But instead of feeling better, I'm a fire-breathing dragon whose fire is extinguished. I sit in an easy chair burping up my motion-sickness, watching it all. I never in a million years expected to be sick from seeing Mama, to be starting from zero, learning how to act around her, looking at her, seeing a stranger who reminds me of someone I used to know, a vaguely familiar stranger surrounded by vaguely familiar things. An ironed lace tablecloth covers the table on which sits a crystal pitcher holding red currant *kompot*. There is *makowiec* on a platter and a huge yeast *babka* big enough to feed twelve. Babcia would be so impressed with the Polish cooking Mama has learned in Canada. Or maybe Babcia is hiding somewhere here? Maybe she made all these Babcia things?

"Serge is quite the master baker," Mama says.

Kasia and I stare in bewilderment at the wiry, bespectacled man.

He purses his lips, and doesn't make eye contact with anyone. "My mother taught me her language *and* her recipes, but that's about it. Poppy seed cake is my specialty," he says, pointing to the *makowiec.*

"He doesn't cook," Mama adds. "That's why we're having toast with our *gołąbki.*"

"I said I'd make potatoes, but you said nobody needs potatoes with cabbage rolls."

"Maybe the girls would like potatoes," Mama says. "Girls, would you like some potatoes?"

They switch to English. Calm and low. Their tone is prickly, like drizzle before a storm. They remind me of Babcia and Dziadek, minus the china crashing to the floor.

I am not really here at all. Although my butt spills across the soft chair and my body is massive in the modest living room, the rest of me—the more important part of me—is still flying thousands of metres above the Atlantic Ocean.

"How did you meet our mama?" Kasia asks.

"Dinner was delicious," Pan Rousseau says, getting up from the table, leaving his dirty dishes there and kissing Mama on the cheek. Mama blushes. Despite its brevity, seeing him kiss Mama makes my skin creep. Kasia's question he ignores.

AFTER PAN Rousseau disappears and Mama has collected all the food and dishes from the dining room table, Kasia and I sit quietly in the spacious, empty kitchen, watching Mama stack dirty dishes in a large white appliance underneath the counter. "Dishwasher," she says to our slightly parted lips and stupid looks. "Makes my life really easy."

Outside, the sky gets greyer and greyer. When Kasia's elbow gives under the weight of her sleepy head for a third time, Mama says, "Time for bed." We look at her, shaking our heads vehemently, but we know we're tired, so tired we can't even speak, so our protests are hardly convincing. "Jetlag," Mama says. "It's when you're all tired, confused and sad from airplane travel. The only remedy for jetlag is to sleep it off."

"I'm not tired," Kasia mumbles, but says nothing of being confused or sad.

Mama ushers us into a tiny room that's a cross between a library and an office. Surrounded by tall, overflowing bookshelves and masses of paper is a futon, opened and dressed with plaid sheets. Kasia is asleep before Mama begins pulling her clothes off and replacing them with Smurf pyjamas. She shows me to the bathroom, where I brush my teeth and change into my PJs so fast you'd think thirty people were waiting to use the WC. If I did it all any slower I'd topple over from the fatigue. When I lie beside Kasia, Mama shuts the door and goes soundlessly to some other corner of the flat, lifeless house.

MAMA WANTS US to meet another one of her friends. How many friends did she make here? Eleven years in Morena and I have only one friend, and I wouldn't want to introduce Beata Kowalska to out-of-town guests. I don't want to go visiting with bonbons and bouquets of flowers because I am so tired you'd think I hadn't slept since I was born. Eating a dry and cold Canadian breakfast makes me tired. "Corn Flakes," Pan Rousseau calls the cereal, to which if he were here Dziadek would say, "Corn? What are we, cattle? Who eats corn?" Washing the bowl, spoon and juice glass afterwards makes me merry-go-round dizzy. Orange juice doesn't make me alert like Babcia's bittersweet lemon tea. Mama drags us for walks, with no particular destination, after each meal, walks around the neighbourhood that I think are pointless. It's not like we're going to pick up milk, or eggs, or vegetables at the market, or walk to church or the tram stop. Here, we just walk. "Around the block," like fools.

"I WANT TO take you to Jola's," Mama says on a post-breakfast walk. When I don't respond, she adds, "Her people have a pool."

What's a pool good for in the autumn?

"It'd be good for you to swim."

Kasia, who is equally exhausted, says, "Who's Jola?" without her regular enthusiasm.

"My good friend."

"Like Wujek Serge," says Kasia, a fraction more upbeat.

Mama laughs. "Sort of. We met on the plane. We worked together..." She trails off as if she's changed her mind about what exactly to tell us.

"Taught together in the same school?" I ask.

"Don't be silly." She threads her arm through mine. "At the same agency."

I am not being silly.

"Pani Jola works in a big beautiful house, not far from here. You have to see it. It looks like it's made of glass. It's really nice."

"Why don't you work there anymore if it's so nice?" Kasia asks.

Another laugh from Mama, albeit a different one this time, more of a cough that makes her choke. "Well," she begins constructing her response, "because you're here, and we have a house, so I don't need to work in someone else's. That was a stepping stone. I'm a secretary now."

"What was?" Kasia asks.

"Did *anyone* read my letters?"

Kasia looks at me. Mama used to have a secretary at her school, who gave me chocolate-covered prunes when I'd go to work with Mama. She had a secretary at her university job, too, but that one was skinny and mean.

PANI JOLA'S HOUSE is like nothing I've ever seen. Fifteen of Babcia and Dziadek's apartment could fit into it, five of Pan Rousseau's house. Our blok in Morena takes up as much space on the street as this villa does, except they don't call houses like this villas, Mama says. They call it a mansion. Around it are shrubs, bushes and trees of all size, foliage and proportion thoughtfully arranged, the owners' very own Oliwa Botanical Garden. Even in the cool weather the various shades of brown and green are full and rich. "Weather has little effect on this kind of wealth," Mama's friend declares, standing in the open doorway. I snap to it. She must have noticed me surveying the property. She tells us to call her Ciocia and hugs us like she's known us our whole lives even though she's so short and skinny the ferocious wind will carry her away at any moment if she doesn't close the door. "Your mama is beside herself with joy," she says, and ushers us to buttery soft couches in a living room with floor to ceiling windows. "All her prayers have been answered, girls. And there were thousands. Trust me. I've heard them."

Prayers? Uttered by my mama?

"You have a nice house," Kasia says.

"I do." Ciocia Jola's smile seems permanent. "It's in a village not far from Toruń and I miss it very much."

Two bulbous sculptures flank the room, headless pregnant shapes, wingless ochre-coloured angels. When I set my glass of Coca Cola a little too hard on the glass coffee table, Mama gives me a warning look, although not a full-fledged teacher stare. I shrug sheepishly. "It will take a lot more to crack that," Ciocia Jola says, and chuckles. "Believe me, I've tried."

From a red tin cylinder she feeds us potato chips that are stacked together like thin curved blocks. Each one fits perfectly, pressed between the roof of my mouth and my tongue. It dissolves in a rush of salty pleasure. Kasia and I eat the entire tube while Mama and Ciocia Jola talk about "the red tape surrounding the girls' complicated departure." That's us. The crunching in my ears is so loud I can't listen to them even if I wanted to. Kasia and I lick our fingers. Mama and Ciocia Jola put theirs in their mouths from time to time or wag them at each other.

Back at the tiny house where Mama now lives with the tiny man, she says, "These are the suburbs, like in Morena."

"This is nothing like Morena," I say.

"You're right: Morena was a development, a settlement really," Mama corrects herself. "More or less *in* the city, not on the fringes of it like here."

Was? Morena still is.

"It all went up at the same time," Mama says, "*up* being the operative word."

I wonder what Babcia would think of North York. She always said Dziadek kidnapped her from her village and brought her to the city when she was just a girl. She hated the city at first. Would she like North York, with its gnarled willows, bent like dancing ghouls? She would like the crimson maples. She would miss having an old stone church to walk to each morning. She would miss the market near the church, the shops along the road, the nuns exchanging blessings in the language of God, bowing to her. I went to church with Babcia just before our trip to Canada. She was surprised when I asked if I could. "Surely you drank too much last night," she said. "Since when do you *want* to go to church?"

I had forgotten about the cognac we had sipped after Tata's visit. I had drained Kasia's glass as well as mine. "I do, I do want to," I said, and fell out of bed.

We admired the perfection that was Oliwa in the autumn as we walked along the tree-lined avenue to church, not a modern church with a fluorescent light-bulb cross like Morena's, but one built by monks out of auburn brick, hundreds of years ago. I gently kicked the odd capped acorn we came upon on the sidewalk. At home in Morena, we'd make toothpick animals and figurines out of the bounty of fall, and Mama would praise me.

That day I swung Babcia's wicker shopping basket. We came upon a couple of nuns in their black and white habits: Babcia bowed and muttered, "God bless you." I bowed too. As soon as they passed, Babcia took my hand and kissed its knuckles. We walked hand in hand for a moment, looking ridiculous, me an eleven-year-old giant, a child bigger than the grandmother who loves her more than anyone. She let go of my hand when I asked, "Babcia, who does Mama have in Canada?"

We had come to the end of a long stretch of road, forest on one side, impressive villas converted into official buildings on the other. Now we stood and waited at a red light.

"A friend," Babcia said.

We were almost there, late for Mass. It was so unlike Babcia to be late. I slowed her down.

"Why does Mama having a friend upset Tata so much?" I asked, as Babcia picked up the pace along the narrow cobblestone lane.

"Is he a gigolo?"

But she didn't reply. We got to the church gate. A Brother wearing a brown robe with a thick rope around his waist was pulling shut the heavy wooden door.

"Why was Tata asking will I be happy in Canada?"

Babcia stopped to look at me. Her face said *See, we're late.* "You have a lot of questions, don't you? I've been telling you to read your mother's letters."

She tucked her chin in. Her brow wasn't furrowed, but arched high above her sad eyes. "Of course you'll be happy. It's a vacation." Babcia gestured for me to go through the gate. I complied. "And I'll be happy when I finally give thanks to Jesus."

I paused at the top of the stairs, in front of the immense door. Turned to look at little Babcia, several steps below me. The organ played inside, feeble old-people voices singing along to a sad hymn. There are zero happy hymns in the Catholic Mass. Zero. Except maybe at Christmas.

"Vacation, in the middle of the school year?" I whispered to Babcia, who was shooing me in. She looked so small, shrivelled and old. She nodded.

"It's just started," she said.

"It started a month ago."

"Not school. Mass. Go."

But I didn't go in. I kept my hand on the oversize iron door handle. Squeezed it.

"You don't want to go to Canada?"

"I don't want to go in case it's forever."

Babcia looked at me, her hooded navy blue eyes sinking, a little wetter than usual. She waved her hand. Tsked. "Who said anything about forever?"

I shrugged. "I would miss you too much if it was forever. I don't want to swap missing Mama for missing you."

"You want to have your cake and eat it too."

She reached the step I was on and hugged me with her small, soft body. I buried my face in her shoulder. "Cake," I said into Babcia's warmth, "and plum-butter doughnuts."

MAMA RAKES the dead leaves that have fallen on the lawn of Pan Rousseau's house. It's a mess. I sit on the steps and watch her, hands under my butt, pressing onto cold concrete. "Babcia rakes leaves at the cemetery, not just on All Saints Day, and tidies up graves of Dziadek's family members and lights candles."

"So, you don't like it here, ha?" Mama asks and waves me over.

A trick question I don't know how to answer, so I chew the inside of my cheek instead. She gestures again, and I lumber over to the pile of leaves in the middle of the lawn.

"I like that *you're* here," I say eventually, not sure if I mean what I say.

She smiles. "That's good." She opens a plastic bag so I can scoop the leaves she's raked into it. "What if I stayed here for a while?" She stretches out 'a while' into a time that several words should occupy.

"Then I guess I would have to be here for a while, too," I say, trying hard to sound matter-of-fact, but my voice trembles. My face feels like it will separate from my skull and splat on the ground at any moment.

Mama lifts my chin with one finger and leans in to peck me on the forehead. "You'll like it," she says. "Eventually."

I can't tell her I will never like it here.

"Remember when we brought Kasia home from the hospital?" Her hands are level on my shoulders.

I nod, limp as a useless, wilted carrot. After pickling in the incubator for days, pale and misshapen, Kasia was a spoiled cake that'd been stirred the wrong way, what Babcia calls a *zakalec* when she screws up.

"Well, even though you could see her with your eyes and poke at her with your fingers," Mama lectures, "you still wished she would disappear, that someone would have the good sense to return her. But then you got used to her, and eventually, you even liked her. Now, you love her."

Who says I love Kasia?

"Maybe the same will happen with Canada."

If I screamed, no one would hear me. This place is so dead.

Mama holds the garbage bag open. I press one foot into the bag compressing these lifeless leaves. They crunch, waffle-thin. I stand fully in the bag, taking purposeful steps, turning the leaves into another kind of cereal. They're so dry and brittle.

AT DINNER ONE NIGHT, Mama and Stupid Serge speak English to one another, which infuriates me more than Serge's moronic, baby Polish. I tighten my fists around the utensils I'm holding, and bark at Mama, "Speak Polish!"

"It's good for you to learn English," Serge declares. "The only way you'll learn is through immersion."

I would like somebody to immerse him, in something slick and toxic, skull-and-crossbones poisonous.

"We might as well make the transition now," Mama says, looking at Serge, who gets a stupid satisfied look on his face, his gloating cheeks propping up his enormous glasses.

"Tomorrow, we will take you to the schools," Mama says.

Kasia says, "Schools?" and she and I trade looks.

"The longer we wait," Serge says, "the more difficult it'll be to integrate."

Mama nods. "There's a primary school for you," she says to Kasia, "and a middle school for you. There are some really lovely teachers. And no Russian."

"Why can't we go to the same school?" Kasia asks, and her lip begins to quiver.

School? We *have* a school. It's in Morena. All those times hanging over the balcony railing, conversing with the seagulls. Those wishes have come true, and there is a lump blocking all movement and function of my throat. Nothing out, nothing in. Stuck. I swallow and cough, but the lump doesn't move.

ONE

MAMA HAS TURNED Serge's study into a kind of bedroom for us and wallpapered it with thousands of tiny hearts, because, she says, she loves us so much and doesn't ever want to be without us again—and us without her. She wants Kasia and me to go to sleep with her love all around us. But I can't sleep. Of course I want to be with Mama, but does it have to be like this, so far from Babcia, and living with her short, rude friend? As soon as I close my eyes, different thoughts elbow one another for space in my brain, and it hurts. A headache begins to erupt right behind my tightly closed eyes and everything spins. So I open them, and stare at the black ceiling.

Yesterday, Mama took us to an Ikea store to buy these beds. The beds, nightstands, dresser and laundry hamper fit into Serge's study like squares in one of those sliding puzzles you do with your thumb. Kasia got a single wooden bed, I got one twice that size. Mama counted money from an envelope in front of the cashier, as if she were bribing her. The cashier had teeth covered with metal and took turns smiling at each of us, especially at Kasia, who she said was cute. I understand cute already. Many people have used that word to describe Kasia since we got on the plane. The cashier had an Ikea nametag, her name was Cindy and she rubbed Kasia's head.

When we got back to his house, Serge wouldn't remove the plastic from the mattresses. He said the white foam would get ruined if we did. Maybe he can just sell the mattresses when we go back to Gdańsk with Mama? Plastic under your body makes the most awful squeal when you toss and turn. Where does Mama sleep?

I creep out of Serge's camouflaged study and stand by the door to the room that Mama and Serge are in. The door is ajar. Mama is in the bed, holding a glossy magazine open over the covers. No hard bound books in sight. My head extends like a turtle's, into the room.

Mama flinches. "You scared the bejesus out of me." But she doesn't hide the magazine under the bed so it mustn't be a Piotrek Kwiatkowski kind of magazine.

"Sorry."

I enter and make a quick investigation of the room. I won't lie: I even look behind the curtains and underneath the armchair in the corner. Serge might be hiding. A pair of man's trousers is tossed on the chair.

"Do you need something?"

"Can I sleep with you for a while?"

She cocks her head. "When have you ever slept with me?"

I shrug. "I sleep with Babcia."

Mama sits up, closes the magazine and lays it on the nightstand. Her face looks all weird and serious and she's not saying anything. She unveils her naked legs from under the duvet somewhat ceremoniously, a priest removing the cloth from a chalice. She sits on the edge of the bed, bony knees pressed together. "I don't think that's a very good idea," she says.

"Why not?"

"Because we bought you your own bed."

"You bought it," I correct.

"Okay, I bought it."

"It's not my bed."

She looks at me.

"Please, just for a few minutes?"

"Come on, how old are you?"

"But I can't sleep."

"Try harder," she says, a little impatiently now.

"It squeaks."

There's a bathroom in this bedroom. It's disgusting to sleep so near to where shit and piss goes down a watery hole. I remember now because Serge opens the door and enters the room, wearing an ugly brown bathrobe. Steam and a waft of menthol follow him, a sickly smell that Dziadek used to rub on my chest when I was really congested, and didn't have boobs yet. He clears his throat.

"Try counting sheep to one hundred," Mama says. "And if that doesn't work, why don't you draw in your notebook, okay?"

I nod. She blows me a kiss. Serge clears his throat a second time.

I KNOW THERE IS nothing to be afraid of, but logic makes no difference. I can't believe Mama won't let me sleep with her. Choosing Serge over me. Serge could sleep in his stupid heart-wallpapered study. It's his room. The wallpaper pattern is made up of rows of right-side-up hearts alternated with upside-down hearts, so that some of the hearts look more like pairs of breasts than hearts. I take my ballpoint pen and add enormous nipples to a few of the upside-down hearts, turn one or two of the right-side-up ones into penises and vaginas. Once again, there's something satisfying about leaving my mark on something I'm not supposed to touch. I should really try to not piss Mama off, to stay out of the way and not draw too much attention to my giant self, but my body is also tingling all over to do the exact opposite. Is Mama going to marry Serge? Will I be able to hear anything from their room if he is in fact her boyfriend?

Middle school?

What is Babcia doing at this exact moment?

My thoughts go around like this. The house is so quiet. I slink out of bed and tiptoe around the main floor; the kitchen, living room, dining area are all connected, so I can wander around in circles like a seagull hovering above edible scraps. There is an entire wall of books in the living room, bookshelves that have been moved out of the study. Maybe that's why Mama likes him: he's a reader, like her. Some are in Polish—Greek Myths, *Kidnapped* and *Twenty Thousand Leagues Under The Sea*—but most are in English and in French, so I don't know what their spines say. I run my finger along them. Right to left, back and forth. I do this for so long that one of my legs falls asleep. Bumpy and smooth, old and even older. There is no way one person could have read all of these. He would have no time to do anything else, no time to work or enjoy himself. He would know book things but not know anything else at all.

"Still can't sleep?" A raspy, underused voice jolts me out of my thoughts. My heart is thumping so loudly it pushes its way into my ears and throat, blocks my windpipe and nostrils. Soon, I will start turning blue and disappear into the moonlit room. Maybe then Serge won't notice me standing here.

My huge body casts a long shadow over his shit-brown robe, his hands buried deep inside its terry cloth pockets. His furry old-man brows are slumped over his tiny eyes. Without glasses, he seems to have no eyes at all. His hair is messy, his face tired, older looking than he is in the light of day. Tata was handsome, which is why Mama wanted to be with him, like I want to be with Joey Tempest. But Serge? Why would anyone want to be with Serge?

Several seconds pass. We stare at each other, except we don't actually make eye contact. Each of us has picked an observation target: mine is his hands, his is somewhere above my midsection. Our eyes jump back and forth from target to enemy's eyes, making sure our opponent is still looking at the same thing he was at the start of this standoff.

I am taller than Serge, wider. What in the world does he want from me? Doesn't he already have enough? I want to shoo him, like a stray dog, stomp on the floor and make him run away.

"Shall I make you some tea?"

I exhale for the first time.

His hands appear.

He pulls the bathrobe tightly around his small body and keeps it in place with crossed arms. "Warm milk?"

I hate milk: cow mucous. Babies drink milk out of swollen human udders. I may be only eleven but I am no baby. My heartbeat descends to its proper place. I feel for it with a hand pressed to my chest.

"I've startled you," he says. "Apologies." His eyes leave me and move to his books. "The floorboards creak when someone's walking around. I'm a light sleeper, so..."

It's all about you, Serge. I would sleep beautiful, colourful sleep if I got to sleep beside Mama. He doesn't know how good he has it. That's what Dziadek always said to us when Kasia and I moaned about missing Mama, except when he had a fight with Babcia about Mama and then he called her names.

"I would appreciate if you wouldn't creep around in the middle of the night," he says. "And those," he points to the books, "are antiques, not toys. The grease from your fingertips will damage them."

I wipe my hands on my PJ pants.

When I start to back away toward the exit, he says "Good night" in an emphatic whisper. I don't say anything, just shuffle off to his ridiculously wallpapered study, tail between my legs.

If you have the hiccups, someone has to scare the pants off you and they stop. It seems the same trick works on insomnia, because after my encounter with the Mother Stealer I actually descend into that state of half-sleep, where whole hours seem as insignificant as minutes. This kind of sleep is sheer, like Babcia's lace curtains, so even dripping can wake you. Drip, drip, drip: water dripping from a tap, hitting a wooden floor. It's coming from the bottom of Kasia's plastic-wrapped mattress. Stupid stupid Serge and his stupid ideas.

I jump out of bed like the room is on fire, and pull on Kasia's arm before she's fully awake. It doesn't take much effort before half her body is flopped onto the floor.

"Stop it," she shouts. "Aw!"

"You stop it! You're pissing your bed." The foam would have absorbed all the piss if Stupid Serge had agreed to take the plastic off it like he was supposed to.

Kasia doesn't say anything, just watches me tug the sheets off her bed. "I can't believe you pissed your bed. That's disgusting. Get out of these wet PJs. Now." She starts sobbing.

When she is naked and shivering, I carry Kasia's things to the basement and soak them in blue soapy water. Upstairs she is still sobbing. Mama's footsteps. Serge's footsteps. Dresser drawers sliding. More crying. She's saying "by accident" over and over.

When I come upstairs, Mama gives me a look I've seen just once before. She says, "It was an accident," and strokes Kasia's hair. "How can you be so angry about something that was an accident?"

I don't understand her question. I can't control what I am or am not angry about.

Serge looks at me like I've committed arson. "You can't just stay put," he says, "can you."

Believe me, Serge, I'd like nothing more than to stay put—nail myself to the floor boards of Babcia's apartment and stop hovering, stop floating. An overwhelming urge to stab him in the eyeball with a ballpoint pen comes over me; I pick up and squeeze my pen into a tight fist and dig my nails into my palm.

Kasia won't stop crying, and Mama takes her to her bed. Serge says he will sleep on the living room couch. The sky is already pinkish blue, the sun pushing its colossal head up against the day.

WALKING TO my new school equals thirty minutes of pondering and musing, less if I'm willing to get sweaty, which was a worthwhile sacrifice only on the first day, with Mama trotting alongside me. Although I prefer walking to taking the bus any day; someone always tries to talk to me on the bus, even when I have my brooding Brezhnev face on. That first day Mama and I were late. There are several treacherous crossings of roads wide enough to line up a dozen tanks from sidewalk to sidewalk. Kasia's school is two narrow tree-lined streets away from the house, and it's Catholic. When I interrupted all the English at dinner and asked Mama why Kasia gets to go to a *Godly* school while I'm being sent to a heretic one, she said, "I don't have the heart to send you both to a place called Our Lady of Perpetual Suffering. You'd come out with a concave chest from all the *mea culpas*."

I looked down at the convex protrusions that are my breasts.

"Our Lady of Perpetual *Help*," Serge corrected. "And it only goes to Grade five."

Finch Valley Middle School might as well be for little kids. Everyone here is a gibberish-speaking midget. I don't understand a word, written, spoken or sung. School sounds like all the English pop songs I've ever heard, played simultaneously on fifty-four different cassette players, full blast. In Poland, I could never understand the words to those songs anyway, but at least I could tell if they were happy or sad. At Finch Valley, I don't know if someone is saying something malicious to me, or something helpful, something idiotic or something useless.

There are other kids here who don't speak English, which frankly only adds to the confusion. We are thrown into the same classroom for a couple of awkward hours a day. There are kids from all over the atlas in my class, but none from Poland. I could be hiding under the living room table in Oliwa with Dziadek's atlas under my chin, closing my eyes and moving my finger over the map until Babcia says "stop" and I would land on a place that one of my new classmates is from every time.

My regular class is 6C: my homeroom. Our teacher is Mrs. White and her room is on the ground floor, near the entrance to the school, so Mama and I didn't have to search far on my first day. When I walk in, all the kids look at me like the people in Gdańsk look at the Popemobile when it rides through the crowded streets: mouths slightly agape, googly eyes, chins out. Who the hell starts school on November fourth, a Friday at that? Why not wait till Monday? Mama stayed outside the classroom, and waved to me before squeaking down the hall in her running shoes.

Mrs. White spoke to the class while holding onto my shoulder and gesturing with her other hand. I'm a head taller than she is. She smiles a lot and her hair is as white as Dziadek's. All my teachers in Poland are young, younger than Mama, and pretty. When Mrs. White said my name the first time, the kids giggled like she'd said 'butt' and 'fart' in the same sentence. In the teacher's mouth, my surname sounds like a person with a severe speech impediment saying, "Was it jousting?" a surprised, semi-violent question. Mrs. White didn't even attempt Małgorzata, or Gosia, which is the easiest name in the world, just pointed at my chest and said Maggie, three times, each time smiling and nodding.

When the kids stopped laughing, some of them smiled and some stared, while others looked somewhere else altogether. I sat in the only available spot, between a black girl and a blond boy. Mama had a black friend from university when I was little. His name was Amazu and he wore loose fitting robes and pillbox hats on his bald head. Babcia and Dziadek thought he was bizarre, and so did everyone else, but Mama said she and Amazu were good friends. If Beata were here, in my new class, she would think this black girl weird, because she's never seen a black person before. This girl's big, and the only person in the class, other than Mrs. White and me, who has breasts that need to be held in a bra. Her thighs spill over the edges of her chair, so she crosses her legs tightly. She wears gold nail polish and her miniscule curls are as frizzy as mine, the only difference being that her hair is pulled into three small ponytails whereas I have only one.

Both she and the blond boy were drawing red, four-petal flowers with green middles. In fact, all the kids were drawing them. Some sketched tombstones around their flowers, others drew crosses and maple leaves. The boy drew stick figures shooting rifles. I began drawing. What came out were some trees, the sea and a seagull with a rose in its beak. Flower requirement met.

Mrs. White held my drawing up for the class and talked high and fast like a monkey at the zoo. Some kids clapped. Mrs. White wrote my new name—*Maggie W*—on the bottom right-hand corner of my drawing and pinned it up on a corkboard. The black girl did the same with her drawing. She smiled at me. When I saw the name in the corner of her page, I couldn't believe my luck. Not only do we have the same last initial, but her name is Althea. It ends with an A, like all Polish girls' names. The blond boy came up behind me, and pinned his drawing up. It said Justin. He smiled. I felt my cheeks get hot. We're the same height. He is also a giant, like Althea and me. There are three of us. I smiled. He said something to two short blonde girls who came into the room. I couldn't understand the words Justin said but I looked at the three of them and smiled. He narrowed his eyes slightly, kept smiling and looking at me while talking to the two girls. They giggled. I was confused, but tried to stay positive.

The bell rang, the same harsh metal-on-metal sound as in my school in Morena, and most of the kids poured out of the classrooms like candy from a torn package. Justin stayed.

I returned to my seat where I perched as if class was still in session. Rummaging through my backpack for the peanut butter sandwich Mama made me for lunch was less embarrassing from a seated position. But my thighs didn't fit under the desk, so I sat sidesaddle. Justin followed me, and pointed at my chest, pointed and laughed. He walked over to the board, pulled my drawing off and tore it in half.

In the washroom I cried in the toilet stall, my feet and shins visible to any girl who walked in, the sounds of my sobs expertly concealed. I thought my first day of Canadian school was the worst thing ever, but I hadn't lived through the dinner break yet.

It's called *lunch*, like punch and crunch, just softer. I sat alone, eating my sandwich in the cafetorium, a space that's more of a theatre for hungry athletes than a dining room: a stage, basketball nets and movable tables. I'm not used to peanut butter yet; the sickly, gummy texture makes me gag.

Outside in the schoolyard, kids hummed and beeped like cars on a busy road. Kids here play bizarre games at break, like one where a ball is tied to a metal pole with a string. They slap and hit the ball until it winds itself around the pole. Or they run around the field with an egg-shaped ball and shout like maniacs. They have so many games to choose from, and most look alien and comical. It's all a bit of a circus. Some kids just sit and chat, which is the same as in Poland. I walked by a group of Chinese girls perched on a concrete wall, talking with their hands and throwing their heads back with laughter. Silence and stillness descended as I passed: head down, breath held, making myself as small as possible. They talked louder and laughed more once I was further on.

Then suddenly, someone touched my elbow from behind. I thought it might be one of the Chinese girls, having a change of heart, inviting me to sit with them. Lucky for them, I thought, I know some things about China and Taiwan and Singapore thanks to Tata's job and his postcards. But it was one of Justin's teeny blonde girlfriends. There was a broad smile on her face, even her eyes seemed to be grinning. I'd never seen blue mascara before. She was saying something and gesturing with the other hand toward the corner of the field where two dumpsters stood. Her words were high-pitched and sweet. Perfect teeth. I wondered if she knew what a jerk her friend is. She led me assertively by the arm. She had a lot of strength for a small person. It felt nice that somebody wanted to be around me, so I marched alongside her. She continued speaking happily as we walked. Kids stared. I smiled at the occasional face, forehead and eyes casting sidelong.

The school dumpsters back onto a ravine. As we approached I heard the familiar squawking of seagulls, which made me feel nice and warm. The other blonde girl was there. She smiled. She too wore blue mascara, but she wasn't as pretty as my escort. Her teeth were crooked and yellow and her face blotchy. There was a moment when none of us moved. Then I scratched my elbow. The first blonde leered, as though she purposely wanted to see only a part of me now. She squinted so much that she seemed to have no eyeballs, just slits. I stepped back.

Justin emerged from behind the dumpsters. He was choking hotdog buns in his giant angry fists. I know they were hotdog buns because I had my first hotdog at Ikea with Mama. The girls took some bread from him, and they all threw crumbs onto the pavement. Justin narrated in garbled speech. I watched. Three noisy birds touched down to feed. It was the first time in my life that seagulls horrified me. The birds pecked and screamed and Justin and his harem laughed their stupid heads off. Something was very wrong with this picture. The uglier girl reached into the back pocket of her jeans and pulled out a string of tablets, each the size of a coin, individually wrapped in foil paper. She ripped the wrapper in half, and took out a white pill that Justin snapped in several pieces and fed to the gulls. The biggest of the birds immediately grabbed all of the bits. She handed another tablet to Justin, who passed it to me. I took it. It said *Alka-Seltzer*. The big seagull flapped and flailed, trying to fly, but it couldn't. White, dense foam dribbled out of its beak. It let out a choked squawk. After some struggling, it managed to take off, only to drop to the ground a moment later with a pop reminiscent of a car driving over a plastic bag. Justin and the girls clapped their hands and slapped their thighs.

I walked away, fast. They didn't try to stop me. I slinked through the first door of the school that would open, and hid under the stairs. Never in a million years did I expect to be crying for Morena, for Babcia and Dziadek, but I was. Mama can keep Kasia, I thought. I want to go home.

I'VE BEEN AT Finch Valley Middle School for a whole week now. Today is Friday, November 11, what they call Remembrance Day. Here, they don't lament war like we do in Poland, they celebrate it, not in the sense of 'Hooray, destruction and murder,' but in the sense of pride and gratitude. Black and white photographs are displayed all over the cafetorium, where the entire school has been herded. Students who'd ordinarily be cracking gum are chewing it noiselessly, absorbing images of uniformed men only a few years older than they are. The soldiers stand in front of cameras with their arms around one another, smiling. The soldiers are smiling because their families are safe on the other side of the Atlantic. I am on allied territory, watching their admiration with Polish eyes, not understanding most words that are said or written, Justin and Althea on either side of me.

In Poland, we don't celebrate war. We reflect not with proud solemnity but with a melancholy chip on our shoulder that gets bigger each year. In Poland, they remind us every September first, on the doorstep of more useless Russian education, how unimportant, inadequate and invisible we are. When we're not filled with dread about going back to school, we're thinking: Why didn't they come to our aid? Why did they let Hitler and Stalin divvy us up? Why do we look up to the West so much when they barely know we exist?

"Oh, they know we exist," Dziadek would say when Mama engaged in bitter war talk with him. "We were the price for their freedom. They don't like to remember that. It's all about Czechoslovakia, Yugoslavia, Romania… but Poland? Mark my words. Wałęsa will succeed, Pope John Paul II will succeed, Solidarność will finally bring the bastards down, and in the West they will say, 'Oh that Gorbachev and his Perestroika,' or it will be the Czechs, or the East Germans, someone else will get the credit for the madness and the toil that has gone on *here*, for decades. Mark my words."

I went through all this war remembrance stuff in September, and here I am again in November, doing it all over, in a twisted new way. Same colours, red and white—poppies and maple leaves instead of stripes and eagles: blood, life and death colours. I'm stuck in a series of repeating dreams. I need Babcia to pour some cold water on me, like on Śmingus Dyngus—Wet Easter Monday—and jolt me awake.

Music starts and everyone is singing. The National Anthem. Althea and Justin are mouthing the words, as per Mrs. White's directions. The old woman stands in front of us like an orchestra conductor, waving her hands and singing loudly.

Justin cocks his head toward me and hisses some things that I don't understand, although I do understand "You're a Nazi" perfectly fine. My throat is made of wood when the words knock against it. Althea says, "Shhh," and keeps singing. Then there is a moment of silence—a much too-long moment that lets me pick my cuticles until they bleed.

When we all sit, in unison, Justin takes a pen out of his pocket and draws a swastika on the bench between our butts. It's tiny, but the grooves of its lines are deep.

I want to have Babcia's cleaver, the one she uses to chop parsley and mince meat, so I can chop his ugly hand off. His ugly, vicious hand.

'My Dziadek was in Stutthof, a Nazi concentration camp,' I want to scream. 'How am *I* a Nazi?' All Dziadek has ever told me is that Stutthof was the last camp liberated by the Red Army—not even the proper Allies—on May 9, 1945. This I remember. First to be invaded; last to be liberated.

TWO

MY EXTENDED CHRISTMAS vacation has now lasted seven months. I have finally gotten it through my thick skull that we're not going back to Poland, and that Mama is going to prevent me from seeing Babcia. The snow is gone, making the walk to school easier and fewer opportunities for super awkward car conversations with Serge the rare time he drives us in extra sloppy weather. He and Mama argue almost every night. They sound like mosquitoes when they quarrel. I can't make out everything they say, but I'm on my way to understanding all of it. They talk about visas and immigration papers. Citizenship is best. And then there is the money, which nobody seems to have enough of. Serge says Mama will have to go back to cleaning, like before. He doesn't know that *before* was teaching and lecturing. The new *before* is cleaning: housekeeping and taking care of strangers' children. Mama asked him once if he couldn't just take on an extra course if we needed more money, and he said some things I couldn't understand. "They're your children." This I understood.

And then they decided to get married.

It was February, a moist, frigid month. The ceremony was performed by a justice of the peace at North York City Hall, Serge without his spectacles, Mama in a vanilla-ice-cream-coloured suit. Ciocia Jola was one of the witnesses. She wore a red dress with a rhinestone spider brooch above her left breast. Serge's professor friend Tom, a real-life Orville Redenbacher, was the other witness. Kasia and I wore our church clothes, and I held onto Kasia's hand so hard that she had to shake me off. I grabbed it again, and held it more gently this time. I felt like I was watching two characters on a sitcom exchanging vows, not Mama and Serge. Mama seemed so small and so far away, trapped in a cathode ray tube fused from my anger and sadness. *Now she will never be able to get out,* I thought.

We went to the Mandarin Chinese buffet afterwards. The reservation was under Mr. and Mrs. Rousseau, which, when I heard it, made me nearly swallow my tongue whole. It sounded so tragic, a punchline gone horribly wrong. To top it off, the reservation was for four instead of six people. I wondered whether according to Stupid Serge, the children or the witnesses were expendable. Ciocia Jola said, "I'll take the girls to McDonald's," and Mama in her ice-cream suit gave her a brain-freeze tight-lipped look while servers in bright pink aprons and jeans ran around her, adding chairs and cutlery to our makeshift table. "At least at McDonald's we won't wind up eating someone's pet," Ciocia Jola added, only into my ear. I didn't know what she meant by that, but I was glad for her attention nonetheless.

While greedy Valentine's Day revellers coiled around us carrying overflowing plates, the six of us sat at the centre of the restaurant at a square table meant for four. I wished I had been allowed to wear pants for this solemn occasion; crotch fabric would make my corner seat less awkward. I glared at Stupid Serge, who should have switched seats with me, and whined to Mama, "I can't sit here." She shot me one of her looks.

"You're absolutely right," said Serge in a ridiculously booming voice, as if he were making an evacuation announcement through loudspeakers in a town square during a revolution. "Neither can I. Waiter!" He shot his hand up in the air and began snapping his fingers.

Mama turned the colour of Ciocia Jola's dress and I could have sworn that Ciocia Jola giggled into her sleeve, but Orville Redenbacher said, "Bless you," and Mama said, "*Prawda,*" so what do I know.

"Waiter," Serge continued shouting.

A teenager with an oversize plastic bin full of dirty dishes on his head actually stopped in the middle of all the chaos, and turned toward Serge.

"We require another table. This one's unacceptable. This is a *wedding* party."

The boy looked at Serge, a look you'd only give to someone whose kitten was annihilated by a Doberman.

"Send your manager," Serge said in an eerily quiet tone. "I need to speak to your manager right *now.*"

"*Kochanie,*" Mama said, and placed her hand on Serge's forearm. Babcia's amethyst engagement ring sparkled on her index finger.

For the second time that evening I nearly swallowed my tongue.

What was Babcia's engagement ring doing on Mama's hand? How did it get here? Had I inadvertently smuggled my own fate in a puffy envelope full of documents in my carry-on luggage? And why is she calling Serge *love*? What in the world of bearded evil midgets is there to love?

As if he'd read my mind, Serge barked at Mama and told her not to "kochanie *him*" and that he has "every right to demand to be treated with respect in return for spending exorbitant amounts of money on ethnic food," to which Mama responded with more loving coos, which made me want to puke all over the table. Unfortunately, my stomach was too empty to puke.

Ciocia Jola sneezed a few more times, Orville Redenbacher went outside to smoke the world's longest cigarette, and Kasia and I attacked the buffet. Upon returning to our new, rectangular table that smelled like toilet pucks and was located at the far end of the restaurant near the washrooms, I promptly exploded the contents of a spring roll all over my white blouse while Kasia poured soy sauce onto her chequered skirt. We looked like we had been in a food fight and lost. Serge grumbled something about children being a disaster and not being able to take us anywhere.

I ate so much the side button of my skirt popped off and we had to leave early because I now had to puke for real. Of course once I started moving and no longer had to endure the sight of Serge sitting across from me, I felt much better. Even the sour saliva stopped collecting in my cheeks. On the slushy walk home, Kasia and I argued about whose fortune cookie message was better: hers, 'You have an unusually magnetic personality,' or mine, 'You will soon emerge victorious from the maze you've been travelling in.' I thought hers was stupid and clearly meant for somebody else, like Ciocia Jola, who actually has a cool personality and whose fortune read, 'If you never expect anything you can never be disappointed.' I thought that should have been my fortune. Ancient Chinese wisdom.

Mama told us to stop bickering because we sounded like mosquitoes and that was no way to behave late in the evening on a sidewalk. Meanwhile, Serge moaned about leaving *his* wedding supper so early he didn't get to enjoy *his* B-52 coffee and Mama didn't say anything to him, except threaded her arm through his. Her fortune of 'Sometimes travel to new places leads to great transformation' was already beginning to come true. Ancient Chinese wisdom indeed.

I NOW KNOW enough English to tell Althea she's my best friend and to tell Justin to fuck off (at least in my head) when he picks on me. Understanding his insults makes me feel powerful, in a weird way. You'd think that knowing what he means by Shamu and Baby Beluga, knowing who Helga and Himmler were, would make me want to leap in front of traffic on my way home from school, but these don't, thanks to Althea, who provides context.

After the most recent insult, Althea and I sat on the swings in the public playground, where we're not allowed to go during school hours because high school kids smoke drugs and drink booze there. Our feet dragged on the gravel beneath the swings. They don't make playground equipment for kids our size.

"You're not Shamu," Althea said angrily. "How long can you hold your breath under water?"

Pretty long actually, I thought, but I didn't want to say it. The tone of her voice suggested that she wasn't looking for an answer. Althea rarely wants an answer.

"You're Salt." She gave me a sly grin. She speaks fast, and in code, and her facial expressions swing wide in a matter of a single moment.

"You know, Salt-N-Pepa? My favourite group." Althea continued. "From dancing in my basement?" We were now swinging. With Al the seesaw is fun; she's the only person I can seesaw with, because of the similarity in our masses. I don't catapult her off with my fat ass, or leave her dangling at the top, like I do to Beata. "It's better than Ebony and Ivory," Althea said, "which is what my mom calls us."

I was beginning to catch on. White and black. I didn't like the polar distinction. There is nobody in the school more like me than Althea.

"We're both Pepa," I said.

"Are you high?"

"But we both stand up," I tried to explain. "Don't we?"

"There's no way you're Pepa, Whitey. Plus Salt and Pepa both stand *out*."

I frowned and hung in the air while Althea kept the seesaw grounded with her legs.

"I'm black, so I'm Pepa; you're white, so you're Salt. *Comprende?*"

"You're brown," I said.

"I'm *black*," Althea said, letting the seesaw go.

ALTHEA AND I DRAG our galoshes along the wet sidewalk. It's June and school is almost over, and it's supposed to be sunny, but it rains all the time. We're a block away from the Willowtree housing complex where Al's family lives, but our heated debate about which one of the New Kids on the Block is the cutest has only just begun. Althea's man is Donny. I insist Jordan is better and Donny is disgusting. "Too short and too thick," I screw up my face and declare. "Long and lean is way better."

"I couldn't agree more. I would have picked someone more suitable for you myself," Althea says, and kicks a rock down the sidewalk, "like perhaps Mr. Pantin?" She makes kissing noises, and laughs, wraps her arms around herself and runs them up and down her shoulder blades. I watch this and blush. Althea takes off toward her house singing a rhyme about love and marriage. As soon as she's gone, I want to run after her, but as I start, my knees make a sound like Kasia walking over spilled corn flakes on kitchen tiles, so all I can do is lumber along the sidewalk, solo.

I was once told my knees are like chewing gum, but they're really more like nothing. I might as well have no knees at all. Huge people need knees more than anyone else—to hold us up, to make us function properly. Althea is proof of that; her knees propel her forward faster than any other person I've ever seen, big or small.

The pain and the noise started after a gym-class fall at school in Morena. Babcia took me to the Party doctor, who smelled like wet chalk. That's where I first heard the catastrophic news that I have no knees, that I will be crippled for life. He took x-rays and made me feel like a robot in a spaceship. We looked at the x-rays together, the three of us, examined my see-through ankles, hips and knees. He said, "Look," pointing to the grey cobweb around white bones. "It's like someone stuck bricks together with chewing gum."

Babcia and I looked at each other. We weren't thinking masonry.

"So," the doctor said, "if you are the house—" he pointed at me—"and your bones are the bricks, then your joints are the mortar."

He called me 'a house.'

"Mortar is what sticks the bricks together: cement and water. It hardens and lasts and lasts. Holds the bones together. But not very well if the mortar has too much water in it and turns to chewing gum instead."

To the miserable look on my face, Babcia said, "See, your bones are really strong."

I frowned at her. This was one example of when Babcia's focus on the positives got positively absurd. (Another is her sending Mama her amethyst engagement ring to make the best of this Canadian mess.) My bones are so strong they've crushed my knees into oblivion, I thought then, and chewed on the white sleeve of a *Tivoli Gardens Copenhagen* sweatshirt I wasn't supposed to wear outside of the apartment. "My knees are chewing gum," I said, to no one in particular, and thought about how humiliated I felt.

I have been made ineffective. Useless. Doomed. How am I going to expend all the energy in this huge body, all that blood pumping in my ears, all those tingles rummaging through my limbs, without any knees? I am a half giant, a total freak, missing fifty percent of me, nothing but a puppet to be operated by a clever hand.

ALTHEA IS RIGHT: I do love Mr. Pantin. He's our athletic and very handsome History teacher, and he looks like Morten Hacket from a-ha, not Jordan Knight from the New Kids on the Block, but Althea doesn't get the reference. He coaches the girls' basketball team, which I want us to try out for next September, despite my ridiculous joints (maybe I can train my knees to be better, like I've trained my temper) and Althea's declaration that tryouts will happen over her dead body. My English isn't perfect yet—although good enough not to suffer through ESL class anymore—but I do understand that dead bodies can't have anything good to do with basketball. Mr. Pantin used to be the star point guard on the University of Michigan NCAA team. "Not bad for a white guy," Althea whispered to me, when he told the class at the start of the year. "But lame for telling us. He wants street cred, but instead, he's being a show-off."

Mr. Pantin assigned the whole class a project on "momentous events in modern history" as our final activity of the year. Althea and I got slavery. Al was cranky about it. She said he made her do it because she's the only black kid in the class. I reminded her of Marcus, the other black kid in our class. She breathed slowly and loudly through her nose and said Marcus was assigned the Underground Railroad, which only proved her point.

We worked hard on the slavery project, and when Mr. Pantin returned it to us on Friday, he said, "An A for the A Team," and gave us each a high-five. "Freaky disproportional man hands," Althea said when I gushed over touching Mr. Pantin's palm. She gestured with her index finger and said in a distorted voice, "ET go home." I didn't get the reference.

CIOCIA JOLA AND TWO other housekeeper friends—a woman who they call Big Ewa, who is a head taller than Mama but still shorter than me, and Pani Dorota—have invited us over to Ciocia Jola's mansion for dinner. It's Sunday night and apparently we are supposed to be celebrating something other than God's day, something BIG.

Mama, who's been cooking and baking all afternoon, declines their invitation at first because Serge isn't feeling well. But that's a lie. Serge won't let us go.

Between phone calls from Ciocia Jola and Big Ewa, Mama and

Serge take turns shouting and slamming doors and cupboards. Kasia and I watch from a crack in our bedroom door. "In no uncertain terms," starts Serge, "am I going to be squatting in the basement of some rich people's house while they're away when I have my own house."

Mama is draining potatoes, telephone sandwiched between ear and shoulder, when Big Ewa's baritone becomes audible to me. (Thankfully her English is terrible so she probably doesn't understand Serge's insults.) "But we need to celebrate," Big Ewa says in Polish. "Plus congratulations are in order to our *Gdańszczanki*. You must come!"

Congratulations?

Mama hangs up the phone without saying 'goodbye' or 'see you soon,' like characters in movies and TV shows do, even when they're not angry and the vein bisecting their foreheads isn't throbbing like a fish out of water. To Serge, Mama says, "Consider yourself uninvited," and slams the pot of drained potatoes on the stove so hard that the oven door yawns open. "Over my dead body are *you* coming to this celebration, or worse, preventing *us* from going."

On the kitchen table full of dirty pots and pans, she leaves Serge a plate with mashed potatoes, a dollop of celery root salad and a slice of baked pork tenderloin with a prune filling. The portion is too small for me, let alone a grown man. She wraps the rest of the food in aluminum foil and shoves it all into Ciocia Jola's waiting car—her people's car. Serge is still shouting insults when Mama slams the front door shut, but I'm not even scared or nervous or anything because: a) Serge would never follow us outside and shout from the porch because he's too concerned about the neighbours and making a spectacle of himself like he says Mama makes of herself; and b) I'm in the back of Ciocia Jola's teeny car with Kasia and warm food on my lap and Ciocia Jola is happy and singing some Polish song and her hair smells wet and clean like summer laundry, all of which make me inexplicably happy.

AT THE MANSION, no one's squatting in the basement. The main floor is flooded with soon to be longest day of the year light and the sweet smell of baking yeast dough and roasting chicken. The swimming pool shimmers in the fluorescent green backyard and even the headless pregnant living-room sculptures seem alive. A vinyl of songs by a Polish crooner is spinning on the turntable. The women have softened the dining room table with two overlapping lace tablecloths, red and white carnations, and fancy albeit mismatched china. As a centrepiece, a beaming Mama adds the *Żubrówka* Babcia sent in Kasia's luggage. She encircles the bottle with six shot glasses. Kasia and I eat pretzel sticks in the living room. We sit where we can see the kitchen and catch glimpses of Mama, Jola, Ewa and Dorota hugging and clinking juice glasses between unloading food and pastries onto large platters.

When we sit to eat, Big Ewa opens the bottle of vodka and pours the pale green liquid—two millimetres for Kasia and me and full glasses for the adult women. "To Wałęsa," she says, and we drink. The *Żubrówka* burns my lips. Kasia licks hers like a cat. Mama is the only one who doesn't make a face while swallowing the firewater. *Sto lat* to Lech Wałęsa, but I won't poison myself for his birthday.

"SOLIDARNOŚĆ WON the elections," Mama says, and reaches across the table to grab my face. She squeezes my cheeks. She is shiny and smiling and there's a new glow in her eyes. She hugs Kasia, who is sitting beside her, and kisses my sister's little hand. I don't remember ever seeing Mama this happy. "It's official," she says. "You'll see. Soon there'll be no more satellite state, no more Communism."

NO MORE Communism? What will Dziadek do? I'm sad for a moment, but then a warm happy feeling grows in the centre of my belly. No more Communism! Maybe we'll go back home?

A fleeting thought of leaving Althea makes me cough up some food, but then I'm buzzing all over when I think of trading Althea for Babcia and leaving Stupid Serge behind.

WE EAT MORE. Mama raises another glass. Big Ewa fills it, but not before she embraces me and kisses my forehead. I don't say anything, just watch and listen, and feel good and human and normal. "To Tadeusz Mazowiecki," she sings, "our soon-to-be prime minister." The women drink more. They speak Polish and say "To Solidarność" a lot. Ciocia Jola tells me to remember this moment, but she doesn't have to, because I am already recording it in my head. They start telling stories of demonstrations and reminiscing about secret church meetings, and they sound so proud and confident, so in charge. Mama looks surprised when I cry a little while hugging her friends goodbye, but then kisses me in the car and says, "I can't think where else and with whom I'd rather be right now." I smile and kiss her back, but I'm not sure I completely agree.

BACK AT SERGE's, I shrink into myself while crossing the threshold. I'm expecting the bombs of World War III to rain down on me, but instead, Serge greets us at the door with a glass of champagne. "Let bygones be bygones," he says to us, our three mouths agape. "That's the Solidarity way, isn't it?"

Mama drops her bags at the front door, Kasia and I do the same, and the three of us tail Serge into the living room where he's lit candles and set out a plate of unnatural orange cheese and geometric crackers. It's late. He hands Kasia and me champagne glasses filled with ginger ale. The news channel is on.

A glass of champagne later, Mama looks sleepy and Serge

starts gushing about the history in Poland: the old buildings, the cobblestone, even "the architectural sins that the Soviets committed all over our country. I know I was born *here*," he says, "but I've always felt an incredible affinity with Poland. And pride. It's in my blood, you know. I wish more Poles were proud of their origins, instead of hiding their identities, Anglicizing their names."

Whatever you say, *Serge*.

"I was in the birthplace of Solidarity on a university visit," he says, "I had reservations in a hotel in Old Gdańsk that I missed because of a train workers' strike. I was looking forward to a stroll by the Motława River, and a visit to the famous Fountain of Neptune on the wide, cobblestone promenade, the Long Market."

"*Długi Targ,*" Mama barks. Her eyes are closed.

Kasia says, "We love Neptune! He's the God of the Sea. But sometimes he isn't spraying water."

"Did you know that he wasn't a fountain at first at all? When they put him up in 1549, he was dry."

Kasia's eyes open wide, eyelids invisible: big, blue, curious. She's the only one in the room who is still alert. I want nothing more than to go to sleep.

"They didn't make him into a fountain until 1633."

Kasia is so impressed with Serge's useless encyclopaedic knowledge that she is making me nauseous, with her nodding and smiling.

"During the War," I say, very slowly, "the fountain was taken apart and hidden. He's a useless fountain during wars, barely a fountain at all, just a stupid statue. They put him back together in 1952, after thirteen years in hiding."

Everyone's silent.

"And by 1952," I add—I don't know what's come over me—"his pipes were all wrecked, so they had to rebuild the entire fountain from scratch, from zero."

"How do you know that?" Kasia asks.

I shrug. "I paid attention in school."

Serge refills his glass. Mama puts a hand over hers when he approaches it with the nearly empty bottle. "I absolutely adore Poland, especially Gdańsk. Warsaw, I could do without," he says.

"If you love it so much then why don't you live there?" Mama snaps. She is suddenly furious, and visibly drunk.

"I wouldn't live in Morena," Serge says, "but I'd live in Gdańsk."

"Have you ever even been to Morena? Or to Gdańsk, for that matter, for more than one minute, on a train platform?"

"The problem with those places," Serge ploughs on, right through Mama, leaning forward—Kasia and I lean back slightly—"is that it's as if time has stopped. They won't embrace *this* wholeheartedly" — he gestures wildly — "mark my words. It's still 1939 in Gdańsk, not 1989. Hitler is on the horizon, and the Brits and the French a no-show. And the Americans? Well, the Americans just recently found out what's on the other side of the Atlantic, so..."

"How can you be so patronizing?"

I don't know what 'patronizing' means, but I find Serge's theory of time bang on, albeit my skin crawls from agreeing with Satan. "So is that why everyone has such a huge chip on their shoulder, and no one wants to stay there?" As soon as the words leave my mouth I want to shove them back inside, as far down my throat as my long arms will reach, because Mama is looking at me like I've just murdered Kasia.

"Bingo!" Serge shouts, pointing his short finger at me. "Exactly right! This grave injustice was perpetrated against them and they just won't get over it. It's always going to be 1939 over there, and the grass always greener, you know? That's why I could *never* live there, despite its complexity and its beauty."

"Well," Mama says and stands up, collecting the glasses from under our noses, "I am so glad we've had this nightcap and figured it all out." She dumps the glasses in the sink with great fanfare and storms out. Some, if not all of them, have audibly shattered.

But just as Serge opens his mouth to call something to her, she's back, standing in the doorway, holding a notebook. "And you" — she points it at me — "you have an awful lot to say here, but your homeroom teacher thinks you're mute."

I open my mouth to speak but nothing comes out. This sudden one-eighty has left me mute indeed.

"Don't give me that look," Mama shouts.

I spread my hands and look at Kasia. Even my pain-in-the-ass sister who enjoys seeing me in trouble looks baffled. "It's been seven months!" Mama shouts. "You could speak English with us, with your beloved stepfather over here." She gestures theatrically toward Serge, who also looks dumbfounded.

Stepfather. That word makes my skin separate from the fat underneath it.

"Hello. Good Evening. Thank you. How are you?" Mama continues, and brandishes the notebook like a sword. "Why don't you say some of the things you've learned at school? Kasia writes stories, about carp and sauerkraut pierogi at Christmas, colouring eggs and water fights at Easter. And you?"

"I got an A on the slavery project," I finally muster.

"Slavery," Mama sneers. "How about Wolfe and Cartier? Aren't you practically Canadian now? What has the last seven months been for? Are you going back to Poland now?"

I shrug. Are *you*?

WAS I EVER AS happy to be at school as I am on this Monday morning, despite the jackhammer headache drilling millions of tiny holes in my brain? Get me away from crazy Serge and my mama whom he made crazy, their carousel of shifting emotions and bizarre contradictions and the trapeze of messed up human interaction that swings nonstop in that house.

Althea and I sit up front in History class. Until May, we sat in the back, but things have changed. We have a future basketball coach to impress and a crush to stare at. My friend tells me about her weekend, mocking her Caribbean grandmother, who's visiting. Her facial expressions are ridiculous and she's making me laugh so hard my face must be ugly. I hide it with my hand so Mr. Pantin doesn't see.

"Girls."

Mr. Pantin puts his finger across his lips. I can't lie: my whole body shivers a little. He's the only grown man I know who has dimples in his cheeks, and the only man without a moustache or a beard, or both, because he probably has nothing to hide even though he's already lived so many years. Althea is right. He is way better for me than Jordan Knight from the New Kids on the Block. "I know we're supposed to launch into Wolfe and Cartier as our last unit, but there are more pressing things to discuss right now," he says. He has been saying the same thing since September, when Wolfe and Cartier were supposed to be our first unit. "History is fluid. We change the course of the class to accommodate the events that are currently unfolding around the world." He pauses, looking around at the faces gathered in the library.

Finch Valley is getting too small for all the kids who go here, so our History class has been scheduled in the library instead of a conventional classroom. "Too many damn immigrants," Althea said once when I commented on the odd location, and she playfully jabbed me in the arm.

"I want to talk about Poland," Mr. Pantin says.

My face is igniting. It must be flaming red, because my cheeks vibrate with little heartbeats in them. Soon my eyelashes will smoulder.

"Poland like the Warsaw Ghetto," Justin chimes in, "and the Nazis?"

"No, Justin, not like the Nazis," Mr. Pantin says. "The fight for

Polish freedom. The Pope. The Solidarity movement."

Hearing all these Polish things, and Mr. Pantin looking at me, makes me feel like I'm at the airport in Warszawa again. A giant *I* protruding from my giant forehead: *Immigrant.*

"Let me explain something," Mr. Pantin says, and sits on top of the desk, cross-legged. I have never before seen a teacher do that. "Have you heard of the Iron Curtain? Communism?"

Some heads nod, slowly, other heads rise up from where they had rested atop crossed arms.

"The Soviet Union controls many smaller, defenceless countries, under this Iron Curtain, which means this: military power, fear, hunger, religious persecution and zero freedom to say and do what you want." He looks around the room.

I have never heard it put like that before: military, fear, hunger, zero power. It's a different Poland he is talking about, different from the one those confident women were recalling last night. Almost as bad as Romania, or Yugoslavia.

"You said you wanted to talk about Poland," Justin says.

"I am talking about Poland, Mr. Schmitt." Mr. Pantin crosses his legs the other way and pulls up the sleeves of his sweater. The air conditioning in the library usually makes it feel like winter, but not today. It's hellfire sweltering in here. He gestures forward like he is going to take one of our faces in his hands. "Poland was one of those countries under Soviet control, for years. But the Poles have said *No more!*"

"Poles," Justin snickers, and slaps his knee. "That's hilarious."

"Justin!" Mr. Pantin explodes. "Can you manage not to be an idiot for one period? Is that too much to ask?"

Teachers are not supposed to lose it. But Mr. Pantin is losing it. We breathe through the same mouth and into the same pair of lungs, one enormous creature with twenty pairs of eyes and twenty heads. Horrified glances are exchanged. Students whisper in the back of the room. Justin's face is crimson. I don't want to look at Mr. Pantin because I am afraid of what he will do or say next, but then the worst thing possible happens and we make eye contact. He takes a deep breath. His weird bluish-green eyes linger on mine.

"As I was saying," Mr. Pantin continues, "Poles were allowed to participate in semi-free parliamentary elections this past Sunday, and the Solidarity party, which fights for freedom and democracy, the values we enjoy in *this* country" — he punctuates with a pointed finger — "received a stunning ninety-nine percent of the seats!"

More blank faces.

"No more Communism, guys," he says, completely exasperated now.

Nothing.

"There will be a prime minister, like Brian Mulroney, not a general secretary of the Communist Party, or a chairman. Poland is joining the democratic world and standing on its own two feet. No more colony. An independent country, like Canada."

"But what about the Governor General you told us about?" One of Justin's evil blonde girlfriends cuts in. "I thought the Queen of England was the head of Canada. That doesn't sound very independent."

Mr. Pantin sends a warning death stare her way, and concludes, "Poland is the first place in the Communist world to return to democracy, people. This is a big deal."

Althea looks at me and nods approvingly. "Not bad," she whispers. "Good for you guys." She elbows me gently. "Emancipated."

"Małgorzata," Mr. Pantin says my name. It collides in his mouth. My heart stops, then restarts with a thrash.

I want to correct him and say 'Maggie,' which is what all my teachers and classmates call me, except for Althea, but something makes me say "Gosia."

"I apologize." Mr. Pantin bows slightly. "Gosia, can you tell us how you feel?"

All the kids look at me weird.

"Your home country," Mr. Pantin continues, "will once again be the Republic of Poland, instead of a satellite state. Isn't that incredible? You must be so proud."

My face has combusted and there are flames shooting up from it, singeing my hair. What does he care about Poland? I wish he would just drop it.

"Holy cow, you're so red," Althea whispers.

I kick her under the table.

"I feel fine," I say slowly.

"Isn't this exciting news?" Mr. Pantin persists.

I nod.

"It took time," Mr. Pantin continues, "but Solidarity did it. Are they called Solidarity? They're not called Solidarity in your language, are they?"

"Sure," I say and nod. "Solidarity." They can be called anything you want them to be called. You can call them The Beastie Boys if you stop looking at me.

"But in Polish?"

My heart stops once again. I loathe speaking Polish in school. Whenever someone asks me to say something in Polish my mouth gets thick and I stutter. They might as well give me tiny cymbals and chant, "Dance, monkey, dance!"

"Solidarność," I manage, and look down at my trembling hands.

"Solid-arnoshch," Mr. Pantin repeats. "Is that right?"

I nod, even though it is completely not right.

"And everyone dismissed Walesa as an uneducated, union loudmouth." Mr. Pantin is now shouting again. "And look at what he did! The first David of the Satellite States to topple the Soviet Goliath. Wow. East Germany and Czechoslovakia will undoubtedly follow, with such an example having been set."

I wish we could stop talking about Poland and go back to slavery, or the Civil Rights Movement, the Iroquois Confederacy, or longhouses, canoes, or finally start Wolfe and Cartier, for Christ's sake. Something more normal, something more Canadian, something that would let me blend into this library, like my classmates do.

When the bell rings, you'd think I'd be the first one out of the library, busting through the turnstile as if the place is on fire, but my obsessive need to walk behind people, to be the last one of the pack so that no one can look at my gargantuan waddling butt, keeps me fussing with my backpack while Al hovers. "What was that about?" she says, hand on hip.

I shrug.

"What happened to *Maggie*? You get so pissed when I call you G—I can't even say the damn thing. I thought you hated your Polish name. I thought you wanted a Canadian one, to match the rest of us."

I shrug once more.

"Why did you say it then," she presses on, "out of the blue?"

"I don't know," I say, and stand to meet her glare. "I don't know why I said it."

SERGE SPENDS EVERY weekend at his Ryerson office, "marking papers." If I fought with Mama constantly and had my own office a dozen subway stops away, I would hide there all weekend too. Mama has her own weekend ritual. On Saturdays, she plays Lotto 649 and cleans houses, including ours. On Saturday evenings, we go to Ciocia Jola's (when her people are away, which is quite often). She and Mama and Big Ewa watch Polish soap operas on video cassettes that Mama borrows from a Polish deli in Scarborough once a week, while Kasia and I splash around in the pool or eat potato chips and play Penglish Scrabble: all

Polish and English words allowed, including slang, although we use fewer and fewer Polish words with each game. On Sundays, Mama goes to church. If a Polish church were closer to home, she would probably go every day, before or after work, like Babcia used to, but because she has to drive Serge's crappy Chevette all the way to Scarborough, she only goes on Sundays. She puts a lot of effort into the journeys: drives to the auto body shop on Fridays after work if something needs fixing; refuses house-cleaning jobs on Sundays even though we need the money; shovels the driveway and digs the Chevette out of the snow in winter, sweat forming under the rim of her toque.

Mama once said religion was the opiate of the masses. Not in a million years did I think she'd turn into Babcia. But then again, a lot has happened that I didn't see coming. "It's the stupidest thing I've ever seen," I snicker to Kasia behind Mama's back when she's getting ready for church. "She can do whatever she wants on her only day off. And she chooses to be lectured at!"

Kasia shrugs, tries to ignore me, a loyal friend to Mama. But Mama always hears me with her super-human hearing, unless she's running late and the hairdryer is on. She looks at me, disgusted. "You don't get it, do you?" she says. "This whole freedom thing, this choice thing? People risk their lives to worship, and here, we can do it freely."

"But you never wanted to worship before," I say.

"Well, obviously I do now."

"But you never did before. That's what I don't get."

Mama says that I will get it when I'm older, that there are certain things that never make sense at a certain age no matter how hard you try to understand them, like calculus. She's right about calculus, because I've never even heard that word before. There are things about Communism that make sense, like the fact that everyone gets the same number of food stamps each week and that everyone can go on vacation, even if they don't have savings.

We can't go on vacation in Canada, where there is no Communism. Then Mama speaks about Dziadek. "Your grandfather believes in God and Jesus, and he likes the Pope, even though it sometimes seems like he doesn't. He prays before bed, says the rosary when he thinks he's alone."

That is true. I used to see him fingering his rosary beads and repeating prayers under his breath when I hid in his wardrobe looking for his atlas and he didn't know I was there.

"But he often had to listen to Mass from the churchyard," Mama continues. "He couldn't go in, because he was in the Party, and although he was well respected in their inner circle, they were always watching, scrutinizing how he utilized their connections, their resources."

I never saw anyone watching, except neighbours. They studied who went up to receive communion, who confessed before Mass, who put in how much into the collection basket.

Dziadek's only brother, Jan, is a priest, and more handsome than Dziadek. He looks like Cary Grant in the old, black and white pictures fixed with sticky black corners in Babcia's wedding album. Even though he lived close by, he could never come over to share in Christmas dinners or name-day celebrations. "They murder priests, and make us denounce our own blood," Babcia said. "So it's like Jan's been murdered, too. But oh what's a little sacrifice for all the things they've given us. One holy brother for two apartments, a few telephone lines, and one piece-of-shit car."

Maybe if Dziadek lived in Canada he wouldn't have had to remove the self-made tattoo from his forearm. He has a scar that he says is from a farming accident, but Babcia told me once that before starting his economics studies in the big city, Dziadek, the youngest of eight children in a rural family, got ready for joining the Communist Party by burning off a tattoo of a cross using a can of acid in his family's shed. He removed layers of skin and scabs from his arm until he was left with a large, meaty patch. It looks like a guard dog gnawed him.

I am not in the mood for Mama's lecture today. She can't tell me about Dziadek's secret churchgoing anymore, now that Solidarity has won the election. Mama and Kasia are dressed for church, as usual: stupid flowery dresses and white pantyhose. Their starving larvae legs. They try to convince me to go to church with them. But I won't capitulate. I'm lying on the corduroy sofa in the living room, Science textbook open across my lap, cartoons blaring on the television. Now that I'm almost twelve and officially a head taller than Mama, I can do what I like. I'm sick of her deciding my life for me.

"Come," Kasia whines. "We'll go for doughnuts afterwards. Baker's dozen." She is wearing red patent leather shoes and a matching purse that Mama bought downtown at Honest Ed's. She looks like a doll that's not supposed to be played with, displayed instead behind glass.

"What else have you got to do?" Mama says.

"Leave me alone," I say.

Kasia looks at Mama but says to me, "You're going to get in trouble." She sings it, actually, and it sounds like a catchy commercial jingle.

Mama gestures for Kasia to go outside and wait in Serge's beat-up car. Kasia does as she's told, but not before she's slammed the front door, rogue flies buzzing in the foyer.

"You don't have to study for your Science exam at this very moment," Mama says.

I point the clicker at the TV and increase the volume. Alvin, from *Alvin and the Chipmunks*, has a singing voice that can drive even the most stubborn adult out of a room. Mama walks up to the television, clogs tacky on the hardwood. She turns off the TV, stands in front of me, arms limp at her sides, a marionette without a handler.

"What?" I say, sitting up, closing the textbook between my

thighs and chest, my arms encircling my legs.

"You tell me what."

"I just want some peace and quiet," I say, avoiding Mama's eyes. "I have a Science exam."

"I thought History was first?"

"I hate History."

"Since when?"

I don't say anything. She doesn't deserve to know that I am so over Mr. Pantin since his embarrassing outburst about the elections, since he made me the centre of attention and humiliated me like that. I'm not telling Mama anything ever again because she will turn around and use it against me. Suddenly I am so furious with her that I want to hurl my textbook at her stupid head, split it open like an Oreo.

"It's Sunday," Mama says. "It's family time."

I shrug. "Since when?"

She inhales, slowly.

"Since you don't have cleaning jobs today, it's family time?"

Mama closes her hands into fists.

"Since your husband is hiding from you in his office?"

"How dare you?" Mama hisses. There is a good chance she might swing and slap me, and my head will pop right off and roll on the floor and stop at the TV. But she just stands there. "We only have one another," she says. "Me, you and Kasia."

"You should have thought about that before you changed your name."

"Is that what this is about?" Mama asks. She backs away from me ever so slightly.

I shrug. I look at her gummy white clogs and they dissolve: tears are interfering with this argument. "You've got to stop telling me what to do, where to go," I say through quiet sobs. "Just forget I'm here, like you forgot I was back home. Do your own thing and let me do mine."

Mama perches on the arm of the sofa and removes her straw hat. Was she going to drive with it on? Her hair is pasted to her sweaty forehead, ridiculous looking, broken up with shards of grey. I hadn't noticed the grey before; before I only saw the platinum blonde.

"You are my thing," Mama says. "We have to stick together, the three of us."

"Why?" I say, and pull back more tears.

Mama's grey eyes are full of water, too. A strange satisfied feeling for making Mama cry floods me, an ugly feeling for which I immediately feel guilty.

The front door swings open with such might that it hits the wall with a loud bang. Kasia hollers, "I'm fucking boiling out there!"

On an ordinary day, Mama and I would say "Language!" in unison. Kasia drags herself into the living room. "What is the point of going now? We will miss the entire Mass. And Ciocia Jola will have to go for doughnuts all by herself."

"Sit," Mama says.

Kasia sits.

"We're not going to church."

Kasia stares at her as if Mama has just morphed into a vision of the Virgin Mary.

"Ciocia Jola will know we're not coming. We'll go for doughnuts together next Sunday."

Kasia relaxes her face a little, slumps into the couch ever so slightly. Only then does she notice I've been crying, and straightens up again, waits for Mama to deliver the news, which must be big if she is willing to choose this conversation over church.

"Dziadek has Alzheimer's," Mama says.

I wipe my eyes with the heels of my hands and sit up to match Kasia's erect posture. No one says a word. It's deafeningly quiet. It occurs to me that Serge's bungalow is so small it's fit for oversize dolls, not humans.

"It's a disease of the brain," Mama continues. "They don't have a cure for it, even here. Your Dziadek is really sick. We have to pray for him."

Kasia pops up from the couch and exclaims, "Well then we have to go to church and pray!"

Mama pulls her back down. I try staring at Mama, studying her calculated expression to work out what she's really thinking, but she's dissolving into the flowered wallpaper. I blink a few times to bring her into back into focus, but I can't. Dziadek can't be sick. Babcia always said he was a hypochondriac; he's probably acting sick to get out of tending the garden.

"I didn't want to tell you until I knew for sure."

"When did you know *not* for sure?" I ask.

Kasia's eyes flit from me to Mama, from Mama to me. They are no longer blue, but black and too big—all pupil—ready to absorb as much information as possible. Her mouth a tiny, sharp beak.

"Babcia wrote about it," Mama says, clearing her throat, "a few letters ago."

I take hold of the textbook and rub its shiny surface. My fingers leave ugly, oily marks on the cover. When I try rubbing them off, I make it worse. Why haven't I talked to Babcia for so long? I spoke to her every Sunday at the beginning. Why didn't I read the letters she sent? Why haven't I learned anything? If people aren't going to tell me things, if they're going to keep secrets, I will have to go and find things out for myself.

Kasia rustles, as if she's made of feathers. "What happens," she says, "to the brain?"

"The personality changes," Mama says. "The person turns into someone else."

As soon as I think that a new personality for Dziadek wouldn't be half bad for Babcia, Mama says, "It's the worst for the other person, the one caring for the sick one, who loses their partner. The mind and spirit go, but the body is still around, doing strange, unrecognizable things."

Kasia is one exhale away from bawling. Mama says, "A lot of old people get it," as if to prevent Kasia from losing it. But it doesn't work. Kasia cries and Mama hugs her and kisses the top of her head.

"How long has it been?" I ask, but Mama doesn't say anything, just keeps rocking Kasia, so I know the answer is long: it's been too long for me not to know. The idea of Dziadek getting so old and sick that he will eventually die is as far-fetched as going to visit your mother in Canada with only one suitcase and staying there for good, while your apartment with a wall unit full of toys, and your grandparents with a garden full of fruits and vegetables, wait for you on the other side of the world. Dziadek should be picking strawberries right now and Babcia should be boiling them into sickeningly sweet jam, scooping it messily into jars. Why am I always the last to know what's happening? What else does Mama not tell us?

"Is he going to die?"

Kasia lifts her wet face from Mama's chest and wipes it with the sleeve of her church dress. Mama doesn't say anything, just sits there with her hands on her lap. The thing that's tricky for me to digest is the idea that Morena, and Oliwa, and Gdańsk, and everything there—including Babcia and Dziadek—is changing while we're here. Dziadek and Babcia seem so gone to me already that I wonder whether I'd be able to tell the difference between having him gone, and really gone.

Everything is changing while my memories stay untouched.

THREE

I DIDN'T MAKE his basketball team, but Mr. Pantin pays me more attention now. Sympathy for my uselessness. Pity for me and my knees. He has asked me to help organize this year's Remembrance Day assembly. "I would like to include a more diverse perspective of war and conflict," Mr. Pantin says. "Didn't you say your grandfather was in a concentration camp?"

I nod, my cheeks tingling again. My eyes dart from wall of lockers to wall of lockers, scanning the hallway to see if anyone's watching. Is he going to make me speak Polish out here, too? I don't need further public humiliation.

"Great! Maybe we could tell his story," Mr. Pantin says, and touches my shoulder. He hands me a bunch of books on World War II and the Holocaust. I don't want to tell him that we're not Jewish and that Dziadek's is probably far from the story he's looking for. Althea has suddenly materialized and is waiting around as we talk, all dressed and ready for the first home game. I nod again, and tell Mr. Pantin I will do some research when I get the chance and will get back to him. I am ten inches shorter under the weight of his books.

Althea is his star point guard (his only point guard). She decided to stay on the team despite the knee I dislocated at tryouts and our original pact to only play together. There is no one on the bench to replace her if she gets injured. "I'm afraid he'll fail me if I quit," she tried to explain while I readjusted the futuristic brace I now have to wear on my right leg.

I was so obsessed with making the team that I'd borrowed several books on basketball from the six-floor North York Central Library. The building is bigger than the National Bank where Dziadek worked his entire career. It seems there are more books in this one suburb of Toronto than money in Gdańsk. I didn't expect any books on basketball, let alone three shelves full. I coached Al on the pick-and-roll, full court press and the double-team. She made use of the knowledge better that I could. Nevertheless, seeing her in the shiny blue and gold *Finches* uniform made me dig my nails into my tightly rolled fists. I glared at Althea and said, "Yeah, he'll fail you, his best student."

Althea is jogging toward the gym. Thanks to the daily practices, she is losing weight, shedding entire skins. She's quickly going from a python to a garter snake. We will no longer be able to share our XL gym uniforms. She will fit into a medium in no time. I wonder if there's a sport out there for me, something that would make me fit and happy like Althea, something that would only require the effective half of my body.

There is no after-school program in the school library today; the place is almost exclusively mine. I spread out my binder and Mr. Pantin's books and commandeer a whole table. I've started avoiding the house since World War III has broken out there. Serge says a divorce will be outrageously expensive and Mama retorts that there isn't going to be any divorce—expensive or not—until we three get citizenship. So in the meantime, they say harsh things to one another. Serge, I'm not surprised at, but Mama comes up with insults that have the might of atom bombs. This level of hate is new for her. Ciocia Jola offers up her people's house when things get too crazy at home. "Sit by the pool," she says, "do homework with a drink and shades." There are two problems with this: 1) I don't have homework when it's hot enough to swim; and 2) I will not sit by a pool or swim in one unless I have a full scuba suit on. So the library is where I hide.

In the school library, the television is on and the part-time old lady librarian is fussing with the returns cart. The jewelled chain of her glasses gets caught in the red poppy pinned to her crocheted cardigan every time she reaches down for a book. She tsks like the egg sellers at the Oliwa market. The sound is sharp. I move closer to the TV, and turn it up when she isn't looking.

Iron Curtain Down. The End of Communism in Europe. The Night the Cold War Ended. Unified Germany to Come. There are pictures of young men in acid-washed jeans kicking alongside graffiti, pulling one another up on top of a wall, embracing, dancing and drinking champagne and beer out of enormous bottles.

The old lady librarian says, "Well, look at that. History in the making. Goodbye, Lenin!"

I pack up my things and bust out of the library, squeezing through the narrow turnstile. Mr. Pantin is walking down the hallway as I hobble toward the front doors. He's late for his practice. He grins and says, "No running in the hallways!" I want to stick my tongue out at him, but I make a face instead. "Late for a physio appointment?" I wave him off, and make for the bus stop as he yells something about 'amazing' and 'Berlin' and 'patella.'

No one's home when I get there. My knee is rubble. I peel off the brace that keeps it together. The gummy Neoprene fabric requires a lot of effort to remove. The skin beneath the brace is sweaty and smells the way dead creatures in a wall might smell. Mice. Maybe even rats. All I can think of is an exposed Poland, a huge protective barrier that kept it safe for fifty years now a pile of rubble, tanks rolling effortlessly over the pile. No more Communists, no more wall on the other side. What will the Germans do now?

149

Why did the Germans put Dziadek in a concentration camp? He isn't Jewish. He didn't much like the Jews, a sentiment he had in common with the Germans. But he also didn't much like that the Nazis put their camps, prisons and torture chambers in Poland. "Do your own dirty work," I remember Dziadek sneering. "They seize Polish soil for their murders and we're surprised that the only tourism we have in this damn country today is the tourism of death. Kids from Tel-Aviv and Toronto, scrutinizing German gas chambers, German war crimes, German dirty work on dirtied Polish soil. Go to Germany!"

Even though I am strictly forbidden from making long-distance calls, I pick up the phone and dial Babcia and Dziadek's number. Mama calls Poland on Sundays, or late at night, when it's not 'prohibitively expensive.' If I get away with it, I will feel so guilty that my insomnia will eventually give me away. If I am found out immediately, something bad will happen. Perhaps I will be beaten through my skin. There has been new violence in the house. A beating might very well happen. But I don't care. The pain in my knee, the smell of death, the buzzing in my brain: it's worth it. I need to find out the secrets everyone's keeping from me.

Babcia picks up after one ring.

"Córeczko," she exclaims, then immediately shushes herself. "Has something happened?" There is worry in her voice, deep worry rising from the core of her bones.

I want to say, 'The Berlin Wall has fallen and the Germans are coming for you again,' but then I realize that Mama, Kasia and I have trained Babcia to worry with our history of late-night emergencies, so better to not act crazy. "No," I say. "Nothing's happened. I just miss you."

She tells me she misses me, too, and that she just started a game of Solitaire. "It's for you," she says. "If all the cards fall in place, it's good luck. What will you wish for?"

I don't know what I would wish for. New knees. A starting

position—any position—on the basketball team? Something to be really good at? A new Berlin Wall?

"To see you," I say.

"Bah, surely you can wish for something more exciting than that."

We both laugh, but I don't know what's funny about it. Then there's silence, which worries me, because silence with Babcia is like silence of a Martial Law curfew: perilous. So I say "How are things?" to diffuse the tension, which causes Babcia to launch into a ten-minute summary of the goings-on of the entire extended family: Ciocia Fela bought a new car with all the smuggled fur money—business is good; Mama's brother bought my cousins a dog—who's going to take care of it?; Mama's sister has varicose veins so bad she can't stand at work and had to be transferred to a desk job, which may be worse for the veins if she doesn't move all day, but Babcia's no doctor so nobody listens to her; Mama's other brother is a lout and Babcia didn't teach her son to spend his children's money on drink; and poor crazy Wujek Kamil has some kind of cancer in his chest, but at least he won't be leaving anyone behind.

She pauses again and that terrible deafening static is back in the phone line and we both know very well that Babcia has omitted Dziadek from her synopsis. I should tell her I know, prove to her that I'm finally clued in, but something keeps me from revealing it, and I say, "How's Dziadek?"

"Oh, you know," she says, and takes a puff of her cigarette. "Crazy as always."

"Mama told us."

Babcia swallows, clears her throat. "Of course, córeczko, of course. So you know," she pauses again. "Even crazier."

I listen for a minute as she explains about infected hospitals and miserable doctors and God's will. This was supposed to happen to Dziadek? There's no point in worrying and overthinking because what's meant to be, is.

I cut her off when I can no longer follow. "What would *you* wish for?"

She pauses.

I wait. I am willing to suffer through the dull ringing in my ears for this answer.

"I would wish for this purgatory with your dziadek to end soon," Babcia says.

The word 'soon' takes my breath away. I gasp.

"He wanders around Gdańsk looking for people nobody knows."

I nod.

"I flip through picture albums until my fingers are dulled, hoping to come across these people he mentions. I thought I knew everyone in his life after more than fifty years of marriage." She pauses. "He's not here anymore."

"Where is he?"

"He's searching. Seeking. Demanding directions to places no one has heard of: war-time, German names. Strangers throw their hands up in the air, when he gets upset they scuttle like mice. He gets incensed at street signs that have names of saints and priests instead of Communists and soldiers. He has forgotten they were changed after the elections. Was that really necessary?"

"Maybe he never knew," I offer.

"Your street is no longer called Piecewska. It's now Popiełuszko Road, after the murdered Solidarność priest."

She inhales the smoke of what is not likely to be her last cigarette of the day.

"Babcia, I have a question about Dziadek. That's why I called." I slide down the kitchen wall and plop my butt on the tiled floor. I twist the cord around my finger. "It's actually not about him *now*, it's about him before. During the war."

Babcia coughs a few times. "I should have quit a long time ago.

Do you know the price of cigarettes now?"

I shimmy under the kitchen table, collecting several dust bunnies along the way. In this position, I can't see the microwave clock. I tell Babcia about my project, about the Remembrance Day assembly. She says this is a good time to remember Dziadek; he's disappearing fast.

"When your Dziadek was a young man, he had a square jaw like a box grater and eyes that you could look right through. His hair was sand-coloured, and his skin became unexpectedly dark in the summer months, for someone so pale. He was dangerously handsome."

I turn over onto my back and stare at the underside of the kitchen table. Dried boogers dot the wood. Babcia takes a sip of something, cognac probably, and says, "You know, your grandfather was a handsome man when he wasn't being his usual son-of-a-bitch self."

"What about Stutthof?" I ask. "Wasn't he in the concentration camp?"

"A civilian internment camp," Babcia says. "That's what the Danzig chief of police called it: *a great employment opportunity for the people of Danzig and surrounding areas.*" Babcia's German accent is eerily convincing.

"Gdańsk," I correct.

"You better not call it Gdańsk," Babcia says sternly. "That was not Gdańsk. That was The Free City of Danzig: *Freie Stadt Danzig.* Can you imagine—free? Those *Reichsgau* bastards had a sick sense of humour."

They detained Dziadek on the street, outside the National Bank, while she, his young bride, prepared dinner for him in their new Party apartment. They were right: Dziadek had been meeting with members of the Communist Party. But even they were surprised, because he looked just like them—Aryan, not Kashubian or Slavic—with his classically Polish surname and

Catholic upbringing, so they almost let him go, especially when he explained his grandmother was German.

"Put a leather leash with a Doberman attached in his large hand," Babcia says, "dress him in a uniform, and there you have it: an SS man. In striped pyjamas, striped cap and a rake in his hand, he looked different, but not when you looked closely."

In Babcia's words, Stutthof was filled mostly with men who were, "dark, bug-eyed, you know, Jewish, like those downstairs neighbours of yours." There is genuine contempt in her voice. After a moment's pause she adds, "You remember the ones Dziadek set up with a phone line?"

Suddenly a head rush. Even though I'm a corpse lying under the kitchen table, my brain is rolling over like boiling water. I always suspected the Brechts had a phone line, but thanks to Dziadek? I know he had connections, but a phone line is more labour-intensive and time-consuming than escaping from Poland. Pani Brecht's long face slides into my memory, eyes slightly unfocused, but looking nothing like those Babcia describes.

"You still there?" Babcia asks.

As abruptly as the head rush overtook me comes a thrust of anger. "Mhm," I say. Babcia had dark hair herself, before it went grey, and prominent eyes. If we were having this conversation in person I'd tell her to stop telling us we look better than everyone else, because it's not true.

"Not long after he arrived at Stutthof," Babcia continues, "Dziadek sat in a large, open barrack where the detainees were made to eat gristly slop off tin plates. That was their one meal: one, colourless scoopful. Only one meal. They were patrolled by guards who looked like clean versions of your Dziadek, and dogs that wanted to taste the detainees' flesh. One day there were only two guards patrolling the cafeteria instead of the usual six. It was sunny and bright, and the barrack was filled with the scent of blooming lilac bushes. They must have been talking about pretty girls in summer dresses," Babcia says of the two guards, who let their dogs outside and must have been gossiping. "They were slapping each other on the arms and giggling, with subjects far more preoccupying than the hundred or so men they were supposed to be watching."

Stutthof wasn't Auschwitz; it was low-risk. It was small: the sea on one side, the woods on the other, marshland nearby, the city relatively far away. So it could be low staffed, with low security. What was very risky was what Dziadek had the audacity to do that day. "You see," Babcia tells me, "the cafeteria was divided into two distinct sections, with a wide aisle down the middle, like in church. One side was for those who were going to be exterminated the following morning, the other for those pending release, because of errors and changes of heart. Dziadek was seated on the left side with the ones who were going to be exterminated: Jews, Lithuanians, Slavs, Catholics, Communists."

Did Dziadek look better than all the men with whom he was forced to dig pointless ditches, rake useless earth and peel potatoes? Or maybe he was just that clueless, because how he got out of Stutthof is still hard for me to believe.

"Your Dziadek had the best luck. Maybe he'll trick Alzheimer's like he tricked the Nazis. They had a plan for him no matter what he looked like, no matter who his grandmother was. There was one large gas chamber in Stutthof. Can you imagine how appalled your Dziadek must have been for being seated on that side?" Babcia says. "With his sense of entitlement. He must have thought, Can't these buffoons see how Aryan I look, how German? I am a part of their tribe, same blood!"

Babcia lights another cigarette.

"They must have thought Dziadek was going to be the next Lenin," Babcia says, "because they really wanted to get rid of this cocky young man. Only a few Communists had been murdered at Stutthof; Gdańsk wasn't the hub of their activity. But they were going to make an example of Dziadek nonetheless. Stop him in his climb up the Party ladder. He'd started with nothing, you know, but since the wedding, he was hopping the ladder two rungs at a time. He was going to be the Director of the National Bank in no time, in the inner party before he started balding, an advisor, or even the leader in Warszawa, before you were born. And you know I had no interest in moving to Warszawa."

"So what happened in the cafeteria?"

"He stood up."

"That's it?" I say, and roll over onto my belly.

"Well, he wasn't going where all the Jews were going," Babcia says. "In striped pyjamas, with his tray in steady hands, a bead of sweat above his lip, he started walking across the aisle, from the section of annihilation to the section of hope, *administrative errors,* where people looked a little more like him."

I hold my breath. I've never heard this part of the story. I had been allowed to think that because of the grace of God and chance, Dziadek was released: an equation of scarce resources, an about-face, and German sympathy.

"Everyone but the guards watched his brazen crossing, everyone made idle noise so as not to attract attention to this foolish man who would undoubtedly be shot at any moment. No one lifted their voice against him," Babcia says. "Can you imagine? Not a soul! And many could've been killed right there had the guards started shooting at him like maniacs. Those were some people."

"*Some* people?" I say. "The Jewish people?"

"Yes," Babcia says. "Those people, in that camp: they didn't rat him out."

"So Dziadek crossed the aisle, just like that, and sat with the safe half?"

"Exactly right: pulled his cap lower over his brows, and shovelled the slop into his victorious mouth like he hadn't in the preceding days. He said that in that moment the slop tasted as

156

good as my pudding," Babcia says, "lumpy and sweet."

"And they didn't recognize him, even later?" I lift myself up onto my elbows. "Wouldn't they remember him if he was so blond, so different looking than everyone else?"

Babcia exhales. "Not if they didn't really look at him to begin with. He was in the safe section, so he was safe. And there were others like him." Babcia pauses. "Plus, you only remember what you choose to remember."

There were others like him.

"So is that why he got the Brechts a phone?" I ask.

"Is *what* why?"

Babcia sounds genuinely confused and even angry. Angry Babcia reminds me too much of drunk Babcia, so I decide not to say, 'Because of the injustice, because of the gratitude, because of the guilt?' Instead, I say, "Why didn't he ever tell us this story before, like this, with so much detail?"

"I don't know," she says. "I suppose it never seemed important before, not like it is now."

THAT NIGHt, after the phone conversation with Babcia, I have a dream I can remember. I'm in a weird lean boat, rowing through still and glassy waters. Bloated bodies bob like buoys. I row through the wreckage. There is nowhere to go but through the bloated flesh, sweeping arms and legs. I think a ship must have sunk: these poor people. A body suddenly flips over, supine like a beetle on a forest floor. It is Dziadek, his face swollen. Other bodies roll, nonsensically, anti-gravitationally, impossibly. They flip over one by one as I row past them. Lifeless.

Stop rowing, I think.

There is Serge—dead—and Mama's siblings, who've disowned us, and blonde-haired cousins, floating and distended. I row faster, stroke after stroke, to get away from this gruesome scene, but more bodies appear, floating up from the depths of the sea. The last one is Babcia; she's alive. She's gasping for air and choking, and she gulps, "Ewa, you have to save me, Ewa."

"I'm Gosia. I'm not Ewa, I'm Gosia."

FOR THE NEXT WEEK I don't talk to Mama or Serge. I vow to separate myself from them.

I clear the rec room in the basement of boxes and junk stowed there for years—drag it all to the adjacent furnace room—sweep up potato bugs and dust bunnies, lay on the cold linoleum floor a carpet I found on garbage day a few doors down, disassemble my Ikea bed and put it together downstairs.

Kasia helps me. We don't talk. She's excited to have her first very own room. Her skill with the Allen key is impressive, and her small hands are useful where my big ones are clumsy. I do all the heavy lifting, while she completes the detail work. Mama and Serge are too preoccupied with how much they hate each other to notice my subterranean retreat. Or maybe they do notice and are glad for it. Mama recently told me during dinner that if I don't quit glaring at her and Serge, I will render them blind. I was so stoked at how much power she thought I had that I stood from the kitchen table, and said, in a really loud voice, "You're both already pretty damn blind," and walked off without picking up my plate. Serge stood up and shouted, "Sit your ass down until you're excused from the table," but Mama told him to sit *his* ass down and ignore me. I could hear Serge railing about my 'incomprehensible rudeness' and Mama's 'dangerously lenient parenting' as I slammed the bedroom door for extra effect. I waited, seated at the edge of my bed, for ten seconds after the door slam, expecting Serge to fly in and hit me, but that didn't happen. So now I know that will never happen.

I moved to the basement.

For helping me set up my new digs, I give Kasia my Europe cassette. It comes with strict instructions never to come downstairs again. EVER. Even if she pisses her bed, in the event of which I tell her she can knock on the floor of her room and I will come upstairs to sort it out. "I will sit on you if you *ever* come down here," I warn, "and I'm not joking. One comfortable sprawl of my butt, and your lungs will pop like fireworks. Your last breath will be mildewed basement air, and perhaps one of my infamous farts as a cherry on top."

Kasia screws up her face. "You're disgusting," she says, "No wonder you don't have a boyfriend," and runs up the stairs. Her panting is still audible when I insert a Salt-N-Pepa album into Serge's ancient cassette player.

I dance and jump around until I'm a sweaty mess. Once in a while, my head grazes the dimpled ceiling when I leap too vigorously. I have to keep my elbows bent so as not to scrape my knuckles on it. When I'm too tired to dance, my knees too gummy to hold me up, I sprawl out on the bed. It creaks noisily under my weight.

I have the power to debilitate both people and furniture.

Why am i such a gigantic waste of space? Why can't I be nice, helpful, caring, communicative, normal?

From my school backpack I fish out a nearly empty notebook—Social Science—and rip out a two-page spread from its stapled heart. I sit cross-legged on my mangy new carpet, random textbook on lap, paper on textbook, and write my first proper letter. It goes like this:

Dear Dziadek,

You might not know who this is, writing this letter, because you're not feeling well and because I never write letters. It's your granddaughter, Gosia. I'm Ewa and Andrzej's first daughter. Ewa is your youngest child. Your other two sons and one daughter don't like her that much, maybe for the right reasons. She can be pretty selfish and bossy sometimes. She used to be a teacher, but here she is a secretary at a university. She only cleans houses on weekends and doesn't look after strangers' children anymore, barely her own strange children.

I'm your granddaughter who is big, even though I'm only 12. You used to give me your atlas to read and you hated when I acted like a little kid, for example taking the cash register you gave me one birthday into the bathtub with me. You never spanked me though. I love you. I hope that you're not too sick to know who I am.

I talked about you at school last week. (I hope you don't mind.) Even though I was so nervous that I almost had to go the bathroom, I didn't stutter once. I pronounced all the words perfectly. My teacher, Mrs. White, said I was "very composed." The poster I drew of Pomerania and the Bay of Gdańsk, with colourful maps and arrows showing the German advance, hung behind me during the speech. In a weird way it was kind of like having you and Babcia stand behind me. (I don't mean to compare you to a German strategy!) On the sides, I included information about Stutthof, as well as other concentration camps, as well as a small portrait I drew of you in pencil. Some of my classmates said it was very lifelike. Everyone said it was interesting to hear about ordinary people suffering during the war. I told them you're not ordinary. Mrs. White said I'm her best student and that she can't believe English isn't my first language! She recommended that I go to the gifted class in Grade 8. Can you imagine? ME. Who was never any good at school at all. I'm scared, though, because the gifted class will probably be really hard and I won't do so well again. It might be like starting from scratch, AGAIN. But I hope not.

YOU SHOULD take care of yourself. Take vitamins and minerals. Maybe go to the Party sanatorium in the mountains in March, and drink smelly egg water and sit in a folding chair under a blanket. Oh wait, there is no Party anymore. I'm sure the new Solidarność government has sanatoriums for people to go to, too.

I wish you would come here and visit us, but if you're too sick, I understand. Maybe I'll come visit you. I'm earning money on my paper route. If I add some extra streets to it, I might be able to save enough for a plane ticket eventually, if I stop buying cassettes and Conté.

Gosia

WHEN MAMA GOES for her twice-weekly walk to the convenience store to buy a lottery ticket and Serge is still at his office, I sneak upstairs to rummage through her nightstand drawer. Kasia is watching *Full House* and eating Fruit Loops. In the process of stealing a blank envelope and stamp for my letter, I come across a Polish airmail envelope with so many stamps on it this address is barely visible. The handwriting looks a little like it was done backwards, with the wrong hand.

I put the letter under my sweatshirt, shut the drawer and the bedroom door, and retreat back to my hollow. I get into bed and pull the letter gingerly out of the envelope. The paper is so thin I can see right through it, all the way to Babcia's living room, to her Solitaire game and glass of cognac. Each word on the page is very round, textured like Braille. The letter says:

My Dearest Ewa,

Another Christmas without you is looming and it has already snowed. But mostly it rains and rains, so hard that you'd think God wants to drown this whole damn place. I thank Him that I don't live in a house so I don't have to break my back getting water out of the cellar like my sister does.

People are going crazy, celebrating and spending money they don't have, because they can get almost anything they please in the stores these days. The old government stores are no more (thank God I retired, because I wouldn't have a job with all the new, private supermarkets). Gone too are food stamps and lineups. They've even started opening stores on Saturdays—all day—and they're talking about Sundays, too. I don't know what the world is coming to. I'm all for democracy and freedom. It's nice that they've stopped beating up university kids and murdering priests, but it seems to me there can be more subtle forms of tyranny.

A couple of the ladies I used to work with are supplying the private supermarket in Oliwa now. One of them has gone to Munich. Now that Germany is open again, people don't have to whisper about leaving. Soon, Poland will be empty like the shelves in the old socialist stores! I went to my supply ladies last week and they sold me a few lovely pork tenderloins, a fat goose and even a turkey. I brought the meat over to your sister's place, but she was unimpressed. She had bought her own turkey, and even a whole ham. So I lugged it all back home and stuffed the freezer. There will be plenty to eat when you come and visit.

I have to get used to new kinds of food, too. The coffee I used to buy is now Dutch, there is butter from Belgium and mustard from England. Herring from Sweden! As if we don't have plenty of our own herring here. You remember the jam-filled gingerbread and chocolate-covered prunes I used to buy for Saint Nicholas Day? And the vanilla wafers and candy-coated peanuts? All Polish? Now they're made in Germany, and people are going crazy for them as if they're better because they come in shiny, colourful packages. They taste the same. Worse actually, cardboard-flavoured, but stupid people are like sheep. Better, because West German. Have they forgotten about the real Germans now that they're supposedly free?

Maybe it's a sin to write this, to admit it to you as much as to myself, but in a way I am glad that your father has been spared witnessing these changes. His currency of connections and Party privileges is no longer valid. He'd be nobody in this democratic system. Ordinary. It turns out that he is nobody, somebody entirely different from who he used to be, a fraction of a person. This sickness is taking chunks out of him, a vital piece each week.

Your sister got fed up and hired a nurse. I don't know what she has to be fed up with. She doesn't ask me what I want. She says I'm too old to take care of him by myself, so I asked her *to help me, but she's too busy. You know your sister. Now that her husband is a big shot with all his imports from Germany, she'd rather pay for this and that and the other than actually help out. She said the nurse is worth every* grosz, *insurance so that your father doesn't end up in Old Gdańsk again, removing his clothes at the foot of the Fountain of Neptune, getting ready to climb in and have a wash.*

The nurse's name is Pani Jagoda.

"But she's not even a nurse," your father complains when Jagoda's shift is over. "She's a hairdresser."

You should see his hair. I often stroke his strands of feathery white. He is dissolving before my eyes. "Well, in that case, she's done a very nice job with your hairdo," I tell him, and sometimes, he still cracks a smile.

He looks like his hair looks: thin and light, barely there at all. He purrs like a cat while I stroke him, eyes narrow, face serene. "I don't like her, Ania," he says to me. "I don't like her one bit." I guess he calls me Ania because she's the one paying Jagoda; at least in his insanity he knows whom to be grateful to. I often wonder what kind of luck I've had in life, that he couldn't have been this meek and gentle while he was healthy. But then the last time I thought that, he started shouting. "You shouldn't have hired her, Ania!" And he thrust his hands to my chest. He walloped me good. I got a hold of him, but he still fought and shouted. "Look what she's done!"

"What has she done, Michał?" I asked as softly as I could, but I couldn't bring myself to tell him that I'm not Ania. That Ania is his eldest daughter whom he barely knows because she left him as soon as she could.

"She beats me!" your father shouted. "Look: with leather straps and rods and reeds."

I examined his hands as best I could, my own shaking like crazy. There were no welts. There are spots, like pieces of amber and driftwood in the white Baltic sand, blue-green veins, like streams that run through the forests behind the dunes. I tried to kiss his palms but he yanked them away, held them to his chest like a baby.

In a moment of clarity the other day, he told me he's sorry for beating Kasia with his belt that time she wrecked his medicine. He looked the saddest I've ever seen him look when he told me this. He said she deserved it because she played with the pills as if they were some kind of game, but that he's very sorry about beating her nonetheless, because he knows how terrible it is to be beaten when you can't fight back. I'm surprised he remembered that incident so well. Of all the things to recall when your memory is so feeble.

Sometimes I watch him as he sleeps. It's like he's already dead. There isn't much time left, Jagoda says.

He always snored so loudly that there was no way we could sleep in the same bed, you remember. Now he sleeps silently, like no air is coming in or going out. I'll often put my hand up to his nostrils. The faint half-breath of a bird. I want to know as soon as he's moved on.

This is not the man that I married. Sometimes I fantasize that

*this is some old man Jagoda found in Old Gdańsk, that this could all
actually be a huge mix-up, and if I look hard enough I can find that
gruff, violent man and have things go back to normal.*

*I want to remember him handsome—in his suit—strong and
mean, marching in a silly parade. Not like this.*

*I love you all very much. Your letters put my heart together every
time I tear the envelope.*

Your Mama

WHEN I FINISH READING Babcia's letter, I sit back down on
my rug and open my Language Arts journal. It's filled with tight
paragraphs interrupted by the odd doodle or portrait of one of
my classmates. Useless ramblings and scribbles. It's time to write
something significant in here, so on a blank page I begin: *Three
reasons to stick to your guns and NOT engage in correspondence, no
matter what secrets you're trying to uncover, or how many adults
tell you letters are important, or how angry you get at your mother*:*
   • You have pictures in your mind of how things were, how they
are and how they will turn out. This is safe.
   • You know people as they are. One way. Original. The only
way they are supposed to be. Babcia is orange—vibrant and loud,
crazy. Dziadek is navy—sober and deliberate, masculine. Mama
is red—combustible and potent, primary. If somebody suddenly
proposes that your knowledge of those people is all wrong, and not
just wrong as in Babcia is not really orange, she is yellow, Dziadek
is purple instead of navy, Mama is green—but so wrong that you
need entirely different terms, i.e. Babcia is now $\pi r^2 h$, Dziadek
is $\frac{\pi}{3} r^2 h$, Mama is $\frac{4}{3}\pi r^3$, then what are you?
   • A person only means what she means in the moment she
utters it. Not a second before, not a second after. Also—the harder
you press on the paper, the more you mean it. But only then. Not
ever again. What happens to that information twenty, thirty, forty

days later? Five weeks? Six months? When somebody reads it long after the moment you thought it, felt it, meant it. What does it mean then, when you're no longer the same person? Nothing? Everything?

* *Find another way not to be deceived by adults. Find another way to do what you want instead of what they need you to do. Don't be a tool. Letters suck.*

DZIADEK DIED in his sleep. It's been two weeks since I mailed him my letter. It's likely still in transit.

When you do not know how it feels, losing someone, you are able to go about your business, learning various volume formulas and gluing typewritten information to poster boards, even though horrible things are happening. Once horrible things are revealed to you, they alter the pictures you have had in your mind, and nothing is fixed anymore. A surface that used to be dry is now flooded and the items that used to sit squarely on it toss and sink, or float away. How can you predict which of those items will drown, which will be carried far from you by the current and which will be beached?

I'VE HAD TO MOVE out of the basement because there's been a flood. Serge blamed it on Mama. The undue stress is making him scattered, unfocused and negligent. Mama said the flood was God-sent and she is glad to have Serge's boxes of porn destroyed, and even more glad to have me back upstairs where I won't get rheumatoid arthritis from the cold, damp and mould. But what's one more thing to go wrong in this stupid gigantic broken body?

I think the flood was Dziadek-sent, not God-sent. Dziadek knew Mama needs me.

On New Year's Eve, against a backdrop of snow, Mama spelled out 1990 with sparklers and burned her hand pretty badly. It was still a beautiful sight to see: the cold, jumpy silver, Mama gesturing over the blanketed lawn like a mad painter. Magical and serene. Winter in Canada is heavy and quiet, freeing under so many layers of clothes and numbing cold. I thought 1990 was the most stunning number I'd ever seen, so plump and joyous. Even Serge sipped champagne from a mug and grinned at the New Year's spectacle.

MAMA HOLDS THE PHONE in her bandaged hand, even though Babcia is on speakerphone. She says her prayers have been answered. I understand what she means, but it still sounds as weird as someone saying, "The Soviets saved my life."

"Enough was enough," Babcia tells Mama. "That was no life. A life has to be doing, confronting, not searching, and waiting."

Mama doesn't say anything.

"Except now *I'm* supposed to drop like some kind of pigeon," Babcia says.

"A dove, *Mamo,* a dove," Mama says. "And please don't say ridiculous things."

"You want to hear a ridiculous thing?" Babcia exclaims. "They've taken my garden away from me! There won't be any community gardens from now on. I wonder if they'll close down city parks, too. Private ownership, my ass. They're going to build villas! Tell me: who is going to live in a villa in the centre of a stinky old city, next to streetcar tracks?"

"Someone will," Mama says.

"And what about all the pickles I used to make, and the jam, ha? Where will I get cucumbers and strawberries? Money doesn't sit in the middle of the sidewalk. Only dog shit does."

"You can *buy* jam. It will be better for your health. You shouldn't work so hard anymore. Maybe this is a blessing in disguise."

"That's what they said about the Soviets," Babcia says, and goes quiet.

Mama looks at me and turns the speaker off. She frowns. She

is breathing through her nose like a bull. She takes the cordless phone into the kitchen. I continue to sit on the floor of the foyer. "Mama?" I hear her say. "We won't be able to come for the funeral. There just isn't money. And the girls' papers… We can't leave now or we'll kibosh the entire process."

From where I sit I can see her at the kitchen window. It's snowing. Mama bites the nail of her thumb. Light blue jeans sag from her bum; her breasts have disappeared under a red flannel shirt. Her wispy blonde-grey hair has been getting shorter and shorter. She looks like some kind of hairless, skinny lumberjack. A really sad, skinny lumberjack.

Mama didn't have to turn the speakerphone off. I know exactly what Babcia's response is. Mama says things like, 'Yes, of course we do. It'd be only right. Tata would want us there. I know, I know…" which can only be answers to Babcia saying *Don't come to the funeral. Right, shmright; he knows you'd come if you could. Of course he would, but not at such an expense. So much money! Your life is over there now. You have to choose one. No more waffling. Here or there. Make a decision. No more sitting on your hands.*

What I do hear when I walk up to give the sad, skinny lumberjack who is the only mama I've got a hug, is Babcia saying, "You can't have it all, Ewa. None of us can."

Snowflakes rest their soft bodies against the kitchen window, covering our sadness for Dziadek with layers of wintry duvets. When I ask Mama if she wants to go tobogganing, she says yes, and the three of us stay out until our snow pants have to be wrung out and our toes must be defrosted under lukewarm running water.

FOUR

I SPEAK MORE English than Polish now, which drives Mama insane, even though at first she was the one begging us to speak English. She worries we're forgetting our mother tongue, and she's right: we are. She gets so mad when Kasia and I answer her in English. But even though I prefer English (I never stutter in it when I'm nervous, like I do in stupid Polish), I still don't have the words to explain concisely what Tata does for a living, or where he is at the moment. The Grade 8 Family Studies course demands far too many details about our families. Disclosure is definitely the worst part about Grade 8.

Before Serge went M.I.A., kids at school could tell he wasn't my father, so they'd want to know, "Who's that guy? Where's the *real* one?" I couldn't blame them; it is obvious we aren't related, like a warthog fathering a hippo. "Men in this family sort of float away," I told them. When kids would press me about my actual father, all I could say was, "He swims." I wasn't being a smartass. That's the word for what he does in Polish: *pływa*. The best English translation is *sails,* but there are no sails on container ships that carry cranes and train cars across the world's oceans. Whether a person mans the engine of a tanker, or performs the breaststroke, it's the same word: pływa.

When I explained to my classmates that my father swims,

some of them would call me a fob: *fresh off the boat.* Here's what I imagine: Tata sits in the machine room of his ship and makes sure its belly hisses and chugs as it's supposed to. If it doesn't, he pushes buttons, turns cranks, or wrestles a wrench. He rarely sees the horizon like the navigators who work on deck, rarely observes the progress of the ship's journey. For the machinists, the horizon is present only at the beginning and at the end of the journey. I wish he paid some kind of attention to our family. Mama is the only one who manages this machine. Since Dziadek died, I tell people that Tata is dead, too. It's so much simpler. Sometimes he seems dead when I think about him, vague and fuzzy, which is okay because that makes him distant. And distant is safe. But then sometimes he surfaces, says 'hello,' sweeps in like a summer storm, rippling the sea, covering it with jagged waves, rendering it impassable. And then we have to wait for everything to settle before continuing.

The 'hello' usually comes in the form of a semi-annual postcard, like the one that arrived today, but this one was, unusually and unexpectedly, accompanied by a telephone call. This is the first time Tata has called us in Canada. A bad omen, to be sure.

On the miniature tape in Serge's answering machine, which sits at the front entrance of the house, Tata says, "Good morning," and waits, as if to maximize the duration of our shocked reaction. "It's Andrzej: Tata." We've heard that tone before, gravelly and ominous, like a militia van moving slowly on an unpaved road, deep, like those damn oceans and seas he gets swallowed up by. "We're in Vancouver for a few days," he continues, "sort of an unexpected stop. Just wanted to say hello…I guess this is the closest I've gotten to you since…" He laughs, more of a pop than a laugh, a potato chip bag exploded by bored hands. "Okay, so hello."

I stand in the door, book bag by my foot, the zipper of my hooded sweatshirt between my teeth, and wonder how he got our number. I have an overwhelming impulse to chuck Tata's postcard in the garbage together with the pizza flyers and the Christian newspaper, but instead, I flip it over in my hand like a magician showing off a card trick. The postcard says, 'Hello and greetings from Hong Kong, Love Andrzej.'

"Hello," I say, to no one in particular. "You sure have a lot to say."

AS SOON AS MAMA gets home from work, I show her the postcard, but leave the news of Tata's phone message for later, maybe for after dinner, after her Epsom-salts bath. She never checks phone messages now, now that Dziadek is gone, and she doesn't talk much anymore. None of us do, really. Kasia spends a lot of time at school, acting in plays, doing art projects, playing soccer and softball. Mama picks her up from school. I walk. Serge is at Ryerson all the time, now that he's been promoted to head of the department. Even though Mama complains that the promotion didn't come with more money, she jokes that she's grateful they built him a bungalow on campus so he doesn't need this one anymore.

"Finally," I say. "This can be *our* house. Sayonara Stupid Serge."

Mama hands me Tata's postcard after barely glancing at it. "Here," she says. "Put it up on the fridge."

I slap it on with a rainbow magnet from Niagara Falls. "Why doesn't he write proper letters to us?"

She shrugs.

"What else has he got to do? It's not like he takes care of anyone but himself."

"He lacks courage," she says.

That's the stupidest thing I've ever heard. We stand in silence for a moment, water bubbling in a pot on the stove. The lid rattles. I pull the postcard off the fridge and shove it under Mama's nose, while she cuts open a package of Hamburger Helper over the sink.

"Look how weird and neat his handwriting is," I say.

"He's trying. Can you throw these in the pot?" She hands me the box of noodles.

Dried-up corkscrews jump in the bubbling water, each with its own small splash.

Boiling water in a quiet kitchen is thunderous. Mama will hear the message sooner or later. My neck is tight as if rung out by a pair of skilled hands. My stomach grumbles, but not from hunger. If I erase the message, she will never know.

I have to tell Mama about Tata's call, but as soon as I open my mouth she says, "I know you'd like him to write more, but he won't. The sooner you realize that the better." She isn't looking at me, just stabbing tuna with a fork. "It's not in his nature," she continues. "He loves you, but he won't write."

"He *loves* us?" I sneer. "He's got a twisted way of showing it."

"Imagine the kind of effort he had to go through to buy that postcard in a gift shop, sit down in his suffocating cabin, write it, buy the appropriate postage at a foreign-speaking post office and finally drop it into a mailbox somewhere in a bustling Asian port. Of course he loves you."

I erase Tata's message after dinner, while Mama is in the bath with her favourite glass of Cabernet. "Don't be alarmed if you walk in one day and see a little red in the bathwater," Serge warned me the first time she took wine into the bathroom. "Your mother's not the suicidal type." I wish I had had the courage then to tell him I wish he were the suicidal type.

IN ADDITION to being a giant nerd now, I am also on the yearbook committee. Actually, I am fifty percent of the yearbook committee; my new friend Jenny is the other. The job requires taking pictures of school events and pasting them onto big layout sheets, which I am oddly good at. I write some of the text for the soon-to-be-published hardback book, and use gold cursive on the cover, like the books Mama used to read. The school secretary takes care of all the student lists for the mug shots; I don't have to deal with her much.

Because we'll be graduating from Finch Valley in a few weeks, our grade has to submit baby pictures to the yearbook committee. Jenny and I begin the photo selection process with our own shots. In my black and white, I'm one year old, sitting on Tata's shoulders, soft sand dunes behind us, sparse grasses swaying in the wind. This picture was taken on the Baltic coast, near Krynica Morska, where we vacationed once with Babcia and Dziadek and two of Mama's siblings. There is another photo: Tata holding my fat, round head right up to his, and I look a lot like I do now, which is alarming. We are both grinning into Mama's Kiev camera. Tata's nose is like a seagull beak, he has nest-like eyebrows. He has my face.

"Maggie, do you have *any* colour photos?" Jenny asks, as I help her sort through the pile I've spilled out of a brown envelope marked *Gosia: 1977-1981*. "Although, these are pretty rad. You look like you were born in 1877."

Jennifer Elizabeth Grant is pink, baby blue and blonde, and Mama is obsessed with her. In fact, she's obsessed with all my new, excessively white, Anglo-Saxon, gifted classmates, who wear Roots sweatshirts instead of cheap Cotton Ginny substitutes. No Honest Ed's or Bi-Way footwear for them, only Reebok and Tretorn. Mama doesn't miss Althea, Finch Valley's star basketball player, as much as I do. To Mama, the fact that I now have 'proper Canadian friends' is a sign that I myself am finally a proper Canadian. I thought citizenship would be enough (which Mama says we should get any day now), but Jenny Grant seems to be a more impressive kind of citizenship. "You never know," Mama says, "the Grants might be good people to know some day."

Jenny is dressed in pink in every one of her baby shots. Her photographs are chronologically arranged in an album with a bow on it. Mrs. Grant wears pink lipstick, Mr. Grant an orange and green argyle sweater, and Grandmother Grant a lavender hat. The sky is blue, as it should be, not the colour of cigarette ash. "Was there *any* colour in Poland?" Jenny asks, comparing her photograph to mine.

I'm a little offended, sad, even embarrassed. 'Of course there was colour in Poland, you stupid cow,' I want to say, but I don't, because I don't want to have to put the entire yearbook together all by myself. It's not Jenny Grant's fault that she can't imagine waxy, coral-coloured rosehips behind gold sand dunes, and fat bumble bees around purple and pink wildflowers. "The Soviets took all the colour away," I tell Jenny, and I laugh stupidly at how this sounds.

She stares at me. "How's that?" she asks. "Weren't the Soviets all about colour: red and gold?"

There is no way a pink girl would ever understand Poland. So I shrug.

"Let's publish this one." She hands me the close-up of me and Tata. "Look how hilarious you are: a perfectly spherical cranium, like Gorbachev."

ALL THE GRADE 8 kids, including Jenny Grant, have climbed onto exceptionally tall buses with cushy seats and television screens and gone on a four-day trip to Ottawa. The sixes and sevens, as well as a couple of eights, have stayed behind. When I moaned to Mama that the grad trip is partially subsidized by the school board, repeating the spiel I heard delivered at assembly, Mama frowned. "Three hundred and sixty dollars is partially subsidized? Where are you staying? The Savoy?"

Althea didn't go to Ottawa either; her parents don't have any more cash to spare than Mama. My stomach rolls over itself like a speeding toboggan when I see her at the opposite end of the cafetorium during lunch. I haven't seen much of Althea since September. I've only glimpsed her a couple of times, chatting with teammates next to her locker.

I'm so nervous that it's better to pretend I don't see her: stare down at the wobbly tray in my hands. The large order of fries is almost wholly submerged in dirt-coloured gravy. I sit on the nearest bench and shove a plastic forkful of soggy potato gunk into my mouth. I can't seem to crouch down low enough. Althea spots me faster than I can chew, and sits down across from me.

"What's up, *giftie*?" she says. "It's been a while."

I look up, nod. Gravy dribbles down my chin.

"You got something on your face," she points, and smiles.

"Thanks. I was saving it for later."

"You don't have to hamster it away. You're in a free country now. You can have all the food you want." Althea chuckles and slaps her hand down on the table.

"Ha, ha, ha," I say, with all the sarcasm I can muster. But truthfully, I'm really glad Althea is here, sitting across from me.

"So we're the only two losers who didn't go on the grad trip?" she says. "I totally forgive you for ditching me for the giftie white crew, by the way."

I nod, squishing the fry soup with my fork. "As if you noticed," I mumble, "with all your basketball stuff."

"Touché," Althea says, and grins. "Well, okay, I guess I sort of ditched you, too."

"Sort of?"

"But we need to have solidarity in our poverty, sister."

I shrug. Nod.

"Interested in going to a party this weekend?"

I've never been invited to a party intended for people my age. The only parties I've been to were adult parties where Kasia and I were relegated to kid tables in kitchens that smelled of grease and cigarette smoke. "What sort of party?"

"A *high school* mystery party," she says, and narrows her eyes. "My cousin Bimal is throwing it. She's in Grade 9. Well, she's not really *my cousin*. She's my stepdad's niece. They're Trini, but *brown*."

To the absent look on my face, she says, "West Indian? Not black, like me and Mom, but brown."

I nod.

"Mystery parties are usually a Halloween thing, not a spring thing, but whatever. Bimal had mono, for, like, ever, so it was postponed." I don't know what mono is, but I pretend I do, worried for Althea's non-cousin cousin. "You'll be Winter Wembley," she says. "You have to wear all white. Can you do that?"

"What are you going to be?"

Al grins like a jack-o'-lantern. "*Who* am I going to be. Someone really good. I have the directions and write-ups of our roles in my locker," she says, and stands up.

"*Our* roles? You knew I would go?"

"No, I thought you'd have a date with Pantin," she says, and winks. "Somebody was going to go. Bimal's had all the roles copied and cut out for ages. Better you than someone else. You're still my homie, right?"

This makes me so giddy I can only look at her and nod.

"We'll have to learn the parts and act like our characters all night long. Are you down?"

Being someone different excites me. I don't speak in class very often, unless asked, and, according to Mama, who has translated my report card comments from teacher-speak to English, everyone thinks I'm an aloof ass kisser. "Isn't that a contradiction?" I had asked Mama, who just smiled in return. Althea is the only one who really knows me. She's seen me toss my hair to New Kids on the Block and Tiffany, and shake my butt to De La Soul and Salt-N-Pepa. She's heard me speak at assemblies and studied basketball and History with me. Now the thought of acting around her is making me giddy. I can start all over again, from scratch. Maybe Winter Wembley's father is dead and her grandfather alive and free of Alzheimer's, and maybe she hasn't had her period or developed boobs yet, and her sister's birthday is at the opposite end of the year from hers, and her hair is long and blonde and smooth, like her name, and all her life is in one country, like it should be. Maybe Winter Wembley is a normal thirteen-year-old, with a normal, easy life.

WE ARE FIRST to arrive at the brick townhouse near The Peanut, a densely populated neighbourhood in North York. Althea's stepdad offered to drive us to his sister's place. I'm dressed all in white, with Mama's furry winter hat snug atop my frizzy hair. It's making my head hot and sweaty. Althea wears a black suit; she looks like an undertaker. It's as if no time has passed and Al and I are still best friends.

She calls the older woman who answers the door Auntie Kavita, which I love, because it's like the Polish 'ciocia' instead of the weird Canadian way of calling adults by their first names. Auntie Kavita greets us with a joyous smile and an immediate shower of offerings of food and drink. "Sit, sit, sit," she sings, and pulls two chairs away from the crowded kitchen table. "Bimal is upstairs doing her hair. Do you like samosas?"

She wears fuchsia lipstick and black eyeliner; she's the most beautiful, grandma-aged woman I've ever seen. Althea and I fill our mouths with the hot pastries. Peas pop between my teeth, tiny delicious fireworks. I wipe my mouth with my hand and help myself to another. "That's my girl," Auntie Kavita exclaims. She thrusts toward me a plateful of samosas.

When the plate is presented to Al, she waves it off. "Do you have any Diet Coke?"

"Look in there," Auntie Kavita gestures toward the fridge with her elbow.

Althea retrieves a can of pop from the fridge and runs upstairs. To my surprise, I am not immediately filled with dread, left alone to converse with an adult. Auntie Kavita talks nonstop, which reminds me of Babcia and makes my stomach fizzy with happiness. She asks me about Poland and compares it to Trinidad. She says I'm welcome in Trinidad any time, everyone there will love me, she says, because I appreciate good food and have meat on my bones. She says she's confused about Eastern Europe and wonders how come I'm not German if there were concentration camps near Gdańsk, and how come I'm not Jewish if my grandfather was detained at one. She says I'm a really friendly girl, and I forgive her for saying anything at all about Germans and the War.

When Bimal finally comes into the kitchen, followed by Al, whose eyelids are painted gold and whose lips and cheeks are smeared with a peach colour, she isn't at all what I was expecting. She is tiny, about half my size, flat chested and svelte. Even though she's so much smaller, she looks older, much more sophisticated than Al and I could ever be. She wears colours I've never imagined putting together on one body: orange, fuchsia and turquoise. I look at Bimal, then at Al, and back to Bimal. My mouth must be hanging open.

"I know," Bimal says, "it's hard to believe we're family," and she elbows Al so hard she nearly topples over. "Even adopted family."

Althea retaliates, but much more softly. The two girls shove and jab one another and laugh so I can see all their teeth. Their laughter shakes the house. I imagine Bimal laughing in the hallway of the behemoth high school she goes to—the high school Althea and I will go to in September—laughing like she wants everyone to hear her. She gives me a big hug and drags me upstairs. "Girlfriend, you need some makeup."

Bimal, fussing with my face, is hypnotizing. She laughs between each sentence. Bimal's laughter and her colours make me feel warm, as though she can, by the force of her laughter and fashion, yank all of Canada closer to the equator.

WE SIT IN THE Patels' basement around a coffee table teeming with snacks—Ringolos, samosas, Hickory Sticks, small fried clusters that Bimal calls *pakoras*—talking in made-up accents and gesturing manically with our hands. My white uniform and frosty silver and peach makeup has unleashed one talent I never thought I had: a reasonably good British accent. There are five other kids there, black, brown and white, dressed in tweed and polyester, performing their roles convincingly. But just as I've gotten used to our strange band of actors, the doorbell rings. I shrink into myself a little. Bimal yelps, "Sir Richard Reyn! Finally!" but she doesn't scurry up the stairs like I expect her to. She says, "Now the show can really begin."

A boy in white socks and a black tuxedo descends, gracefully navigating the carpeted stairs, our very own basement royalty. His hair is shiny and black, like Bimal's, but coiffed into a single large curl atop his broad forehead. He pauses at the bottom, waits until we look at him, bows and unleashes a cascade of hand gestures. He should be wearing a cape and a sword.

"Sir Richard!" Bimal squeals. "You've arrived." She kisses him on both cheeks, or rather kisses the air in the vicinity of his cheeks. "Okay, to break from character for a sec," Bimal says, now holding the boy's hand, "this is my dear friend David Gross. David, you know everyone, except Gosia."

David is beautiful and my Polish name sounds so ugly next to him.

"Maggie," I correct Bimal. Althea shoots me one of her looks.

David immediately lets go of Bimal's hand and bows before me like the Prince in the illustrated Hans Christian Andersen volumes Mama read to me when I was little. Except he isn't going for my foot with a glass slipper, he is going for my hand. If I were standing, I'd be towering over poor David like the Giant over Jack.

"*Jolie Marguerite,*" he says, and kisses my hand. I immediately pull it away from him and hide it behind my back.

"Ahem," Bimal interrupts. "Winter. Winter Wembley *pour ce soir, señor.*"

David ignores her, bows once more. "*Enchanté.* You are the most beautiful Snow Queen."

In an instant, with tea lights glowing behind him, Boyz II Men softly crooning around us, the buzz of conversation dying, I am transformed into Winter Wembley: skinny, average height, smooth-haired, Anglo-Saxon Goddess. At this moment I am as beautiful to David as Jenny Grant is to everyone else. I feel so good that I could probably run laps around the gym and make the basketball team. David has used the unthinkable word to describe me: beautiful.

BIMAL AND I and a couple of other girls at the party have exchanged phone numbers, a move that caused Althea to frown. Later in the car, when I asked why she cared, she said she was tired, that's all. "I'll always be your friend," I told her, "no matter how many other people I'm friends with, or what class I'm in, okay?"

"Like you were friends with me when Jen Grant came on the scene?"

Thank God the car was dark so my red face didn't give away my hurt and embarrassment.

"You don't have to get all sentimental. I can tell you have a crush on David."

"Do not," I said, quietly appalled.

"Of course you do," she said, "but you should know that he is *gay.*"

"Al!" I squealed, gesturing with raised eyebrows toward her stepdad.

"Relax. Vineet's deaf," Althea said. "David Gross is as gay as the lederhosen-wearing boys in *The Sound of Music.*"

I didn't know what she meant. "Whatever," I said.

"Not whatever, *homegirl*," Althea said, and little bits of spit came flying out of her mouth. "He doesn't want what you got. He wants dick in his corn hole."

"Ee-eew, that's disgusting." I was used to being shocked by the things Althea said, but this was of a whole different order. "Are you making this up?"

"As if I could make that up: Mr. Gross Gross."

An image of exactly what she had described appeared in my head. "Oh. My. God. You are such a pervert. That is almost as gross as a BJ."

"Way grosser," she exclaimed. "And I'm not the pervert. David is the pervert."

David Gross, who told me I'm beautiful? Perverts don't say things like that. David is a boy who might want to kiss me, in spite of all my genetic flaws.

I'VE BEEN THINKING about David for a couple of days now. He's no Michael Jordan, with his sinewy arms and sculpted cheekbones, or Jordan Knight with his perfect hair and beautiful teeth, but he is David, smouldering and mysterious. I think about him rather than dead Dziadek, or lonely Babcia, or sad Mama, or absent Serge, or Tata's writing and not-writing from somewhere in the middle of an ocean. The idea of David makes me feel like I could take Babcia's advice and choose here. What other choice do I have?

"DID YOU FORGET to tell me something?" Mama says one day, as I'm sitting around daydreaming about David, her face painting me guilty instead of forgetful.

"Forget to tell you what?"

"Any messages you might have accidentally erased in the last day or two?" she asks, her face still doing it: guilty until proven innocent.

"Why are you asking *me*?" I say. "Ask Kasia. She always erases Jen and Al's messages."

"Do not!" Kasia shouts from the living room.

"It's not Jenny's messages I'm after," Mama says.

Mama approaches the machine in the foyer, presses play. Tata's voice fills the house. "Hello again. It's Andrzej. I've decided I shouldn't waste this opportunity, so I will just go ahead without hearing back from you. The firm will pay, so I'll fly to Toronto for a day. Tomorrow, late morning." He rhymes off a phone number and adds, "Call, if you're absolutely opposed to the idea."

"Tata's coming!" Kasia shouts.

"Would you have erased this one, too?" Mama says, hands on hips, one foot forward, like a horse, as if she'll kick me. "And then what? I would've answered the door expecting the mailman, and surprise!" She throws her hands up in the air.

My mother is not one for physical violence. She fights with words and placards. I was too young at the time to remember all the demonstrations Mama took part in, strikes she supported. I know there were people who threw glass and stink bombs at the militia, because Dziadek had rumbled about it while reading his twice-daily newspapers, but Mama was not one of them. She didn't hurt people. She rallied her students, typed up leaflets, got them printed in the back of questionable shops that sold paint or shoes up front, herded teenagers in front of government buildings and Soviet monuments. She believed in Solidarity, although Solidarity didn't believe in her. "Wałęsa is a bible thumper," she'd say. "He doesn't need a heretic like me in the ranks." Now that Canada has converted Mama into an avid churchgoer, she thinks *Communism* was the opiate of the masses, and church was just somewhere to meet.

"So you want your father to confront me, is that it?" Mama says. "Pounce on me?"

Mama stands there, swaying, eyes wide open, waiting for me

to say something She raises her hand.

I flinch.

Her face softens. "You didn't think I was going to hit you?"

I shrug.

"Maybe I'll propose that the two of us meet at the Polish church in Mississauga," Mama says. "It's close to the airport. I don't want him in this house."

"Maybe you could meet him at a coffee shop," I say.

"Like a date?" Mama scoffs.

When the phone rings, I jump, as if Tata himself has just popped out of the coat closet. My heart has sped up from a few beats to a million, pumping hugely in my throat. Mama picks up the phone, then hands me the receiver. "It's for you." I have to wipe my sweaty hands on my shorts before I can properly grasp the phone.

"Hello?" I say, so slowly that the single word takes time. My hands shake uncontrollably.

"Yo, it's Bimal."

My heart goes from ten to zero: stops dead in mid-pulse. I shoo Mama away angrily. Bimal is almost as good as David. Maybe she has a message from David. Maybe he's too nervous to call himself.

Mama goes outside to water the fat peonies that grow along the driveway, while Bimal makes stupid small talk. Then she says, "Let's cut to the chase."

I nod.

"David doesn't reciprocate the feelings. He doesn't want to go out with you. I shouldn't really be telling you this, but you're Al's friend and I believe in being as honest as I was at David's when I told him about you, *the crush*, and so was his mom, and he said okay but his mom said you're *Polish*."

"I'm almost Canadian, like all of you guys."

"Well..." Bimal hesitates. "She said Polish might as well be Nazi. And he can't go out with a Pole because he's Jewish. His mom said his grandparents—those who weren't murdered at Auschwitz—would turn over in their graves if he went out with you."

Mama is walking barefoot through the long grass of the wet lawn. I feel sick to my stomach. It's so hot and humid in the house it feels more like early August than early June. It's hard to breathe. People die of asthma when the weather's like this.

"But I'm not German."

"You're not a *Nazi*, you mean," Bimal says. "Not all Germans were Nazis."

"Whatever. I'm not a Nazi and I'm not German. And I'm not a Pole anymore."

"The Nazis gassed half of David's family, *in* Poland, and drove the other half out of their homeland, but it was the Poles who rounded them all up into the Warsaw Ghetto in the first place. *Hello?*"

WHEN I CRY on the sleeve of Mama's Dire Straits t-shirt on the front steps of Serge's bungalow, the June sunshine heating my bare legs, Mama presses my head to her shoulder and rocks us gently, back and forth. She kisses my head and rubs the rough skin of my upper arm so rhythmically that she lulls me into a soft half-sleep. She is quiet, reassuring. When I stop hiccupping from all the tears, she finally says, "I can't really blame him though."

I eject myself from her grasp.

"Don't look at me like that," she says. "You can't blame him. Would you go out with a German?"

"Not all Germans were Nazis," I say.

"Fair enough, but would you? Would you go out with that Justin Schmitt from your old class?"

"He's an asshole," I say, "and a bully."

"If he *weren't* a bully?"

I shrug.

"Then he'd still be of German origin, and you still wouldn't go out with him."

The thought of kissing Justin Shit makes my teeth hurt.

"We've done a lot of bad things to one another," Mama says, "and to the Jews. Germans, Poles, Russians: it was all a mess. Some people intervened, but most didn't. They just let it happen. The Nazis didn't make us do everything, Gosia. They just let it happen. When in '68 Comrade Gomułka carried out his *Czystka*—the Cleansing—and expelled Polish Jews to Israel, everyone thought it was logical, fair and expected. 'Now they have their own land. Why not?' Poles did that. I was your age when that happened."

Mama is raising her voice now. "Poles did that, on their own, not because Hitler told them to, and they obeyed him to save their own butts, but they had a choice. My friend Mira Szulman from down the hall thought of me very differently after the Czystka."

I press my chest to my knees, the concrete steps impossibly hard under my sitz bones, and fold myself into a compact ball. My toes are so long and spaced out that I can interlace fingers and toes, which I do. Stupid body tricks to distract my brain, messed up thoughts firing in all directions.

"My point is," Mama says, turning to me, "people don't forget those kinds of injustices. David's family hasn't forgotten. Ours hasn't. No one does. It's in our bones."

"It's 1991," I mumble, mouth against warm knees, "get over it."

"We can't get over it. We don't forget. We may ignore, store these injustices for later, but we don't forget. Sooner or later it comes back, affects present decisions that have little to do with those past injustices."

Now she's speaking Japanese. I have no idea what Mama is talking about. But I do know that David won't go out with me. And why would he go out with a 13-year-old Grade 8 giant, with boobs and enough fat to smother a small man; with bad joints, frizzy hair and no father, even though she did look beautiful in a certain light dressed like the Snow Queen, all in white.

IT'S EVENING, and the telephone rings. I am completely numb. I don't start. I don't care. I just lie on the couch and don't even lift my head. Mama talks into the phone for a long while, the hum of the conversation low and constant while Kasia watches TV. Mama pokes her head into the living room just as the next show—*Growing Pains*—starts, and says, "The ship leaves port sooner than he thought, so he's not coming after all. Who wants to say hello?"

Kasia knocks over a chair as she leaps from the table, bony heels hitting hardwood. I turn up the volume and roll onto my elbow.

FIVE

I AM HUGE NOW, the size of a proper man. Though I haven't been with any men at nineteen, that's not David's fault.

Not long after Bimal's phone call squashed my 13-year-old heart into a cow patty, I ran into David at a mutual friend's birthday party at the Bowlerama. When I tried avoiding him by lining up for a pop at the bar, he followed me and cornered me into a conversation by the coatracks. "It's the seventh and final day of my grandfather's shiva," he said, and went from pink to purple to green in the face of the intense strobe lights. "I had to get out of our house."

I nodded.

"You know what a shiva is?"

I nodded once more. I had read about Judaism since Bimal's phone call, since my project about Dziadek and the information Babcia gave me, since my conversation with Mama about the Czystka. "I know you shouldn't be *here* if it's the last day of your grandfather's shiva," I said to David.

"Bimal told me your grandfather died, too," he said, and looked down at his hands. He was scrawny in his Blind Melon t-shirt and Roots sweatpants, a little kid, whereas I was an old teenager in baggy Dickies overalls and Doc Martens boots. "We have a lot in common, you and I."

My heart jumped like the bowling ball Althea had just tossed onto a lane some distance away. "We do?"

"Yeah." He looked right at me. His face was perfectly smooth and pale. I wondered when he'd begin growing facial hair. It felt a little weird to be so attracted to someone who now appeared so juvenile. "I'm not a WASP, like you. I get the whole Euro thing, the latkes, the copious amounts of cabbage." He grinned. "The contradictions," and gestured toward my cherry boots and the De La Soul 'Me, Myself and I' t-shirt I was wearing.

"Touché," I said, and clasped closed the side of my overalls that was hanging down between my legs. It now covered up the t-shirt logo.

"The racist grandparents," David continued.

I frowned.

I didn't think of Babcia and Dziadek as racist so much as misguided. But he had a point. He pulled on my arm and lowered me to sit down on a bench. He had bought two Cokes, which we sipped through skinny straws that multiplied the bubbles tenfold and made us burp nonstop. "Listen: I know what Bimal told you, and it's partially true."

My heart jumped again, but this time splintered into ten even pieces upon landing.

"I'm not gay. I do think you're beautiful, but I'm just not ready for all that relationship stuff."

He watched me for a moment: I didn't move, I didn't breathe, didn't blink.

"I'm a nerd, a freak like you. I think we'd make great friends."

"Thanks a lot," I said, buoyed by the sugar and caffeine. "Every girl loves to be called a nerd and a freak, all in one breath."

He punched my arm lightly. "You know what I mean."

I did.

We laughed. We talked. We even bowled a little between retreating onto our bench by the coatracks and talking some more. We talked about our families, our absentee fathers. His was a renowned plastic surgeon who travelled around the country and lectured. We did have a lot in common. After an abridged version of my story, David said, "I sense you still have a lot of admiration for your father's athleticism…"

Despite me shaking my head vehemently, he added, "And a lot of fury over his abandonment of you."

David wasn't a little kid at all; he was an old man in a little kid's body.

"His decathlon is all great and stuff, but it's better to do one thing well than ten things in a mediocre way. He doesn't sound that great to me. In fact, his kind of scattered approach is what made him such a commitment phobe, like me." He laughed at that, while I thought about his words, about one thing being better than ten, about people's insistence on committing to one thing as opposed to straddling two, or dabbling in many.

I took those words, and grew with them.

In middle school, Althea and I were identical sizes, towering over David, Bimal, and all other friends, but in high school I hit an unexpected growth spurt, one brought on by the death of my beloved Babcia.

ONCE BABCIA is gone, my root system is completely severed and my body makes straight for the skies in an attempt to be with her. Perhaps Althea grew also; perhaps I will find out one day. At nineteen, I am over six feet tall, and so muscular nothing jiggles anymore. A high school gym teacher suggested I try rowing, make the most of my size and strength, especially my upper body strength. Rowing became my one thing; this one replaced the need for many.

Rowing and a double knee replacement have transformed my body from one resembling a house to one more akin to the single scull in which I move through Lake Ontario each morning at

5:15 AM. I love being awake when the rest of the world's asleep. Nothing can surprise me. Blood flowing, muscles elastic, mind sharpened. I've gotten used to the burn in my shins, thighs and shoulders. It rarely feels like flesh separating from bone anymore, just complete cellular awareness: everything works, everything moves, everything improves, even if plastic and metal hold it all together. No more chewing gum. It's just me and the water: no teammates, no spectators, no family. Fish breathing beneath, seagulls soaring above, organisms growing and expiring. Me—half fish, half human—participating in it all. Doing. Confronting.

The coach at a safe distance away times my progress from the clubhouse. I move farther and farther west each day, improving my time and practising my escape from Toronto.

"WHAT AM I going to do when you're gone?" Mama says, as we walk down Bloor Street West in the early evening. "Who's going to protect your old mother?"

Kasia, who is walking ahead of us, turns around and flashes a half smile. To her Mama says, "We're going to have to get a big nasty Doberman, eh?"

"Maybe you could pick another breed," I suggest. "Or no breed at all. Mongrels are best."

'Flawed, and more faithful, and real,' I want to add, but I don't have to because Mama reaches to stroke my cheek and kiss me.

A flower shop owner hoses down the sidewalk several paces ahead of us. Green plastic buckets filled with massive sunflowers rumble on the asphalt from the ricochet of the hose's powerful stream. The smell of water on hot pavement makes me dizzy. Tomorrow, I'll be leaving this place. The street is a river, and Mama, Kasia and I are floating westbound on a stray lily pad, edging closer to where I'm going, closer to goodbye. Leftover June bugs jump like popcorn out of nowhere, silly anti-gravitational insects. "Relentless little fuckers," Kasia says all of a sudden, and ducks. "It's the end of August. Die already."

I swat one away, but I won't let us miss a step. We can't slow down. I nearly peel Kasia's sneakers off her heels as I plough on.

"Watch it, Cyborg," she yelps.

"God, we're going to miss you," Mama says, and squeezes my arm.

My bicep tightens and stiffens under Mama's touch, too firm for her softness. I have long ago replaced my own softness with methodical workouts, an impatient stopwatch and obstinate strokes of the oars, filled my longing for people with exertion of my body. I thank my guardian angels Babcia and Dziadek up in the sky every day for physical exercise, the pursuit of it: it has saved my life, I am convinced of that.

"You won't miss me," I say, and gesture toward Kasia with my chin. "Kasia's already planning her takeover of my room."

"I don't want your room," Kasia says, without turning around.

"*I'll* be taking your room," Mama says quietly, and gives me a somewhat reprimanding look. For the past five years Mama's been sleeping in the living room of our rented Lakeshore apartment on a Polish-made foldout sofa that sounds like a World War II train grinding to a halt every time it's opened and closed. When Mama and Serge split for good, I stomped my feet about the small, neglected apartment we were moving to, as well as the lousy west end high school Mama had enrolled me in. "I don't understand you," Mama had shouted. "I thought you despise Serge. I thought you'd be glad to be far away from him." But far away from Serge also meant far away from Althea, Bimal and David, who stayed behind in North York. I wonder if Althea is living out the plan we had designed for ourselves, playing basketball and being offered American university scholarships for her unbelievable three-point shot.

"Do you remember how you wouldn't speak to me for all of Grade 9 because I wouldn't let you enrol at North York Central

191

and live at Althea's, like you wanted to? Can you imagine if you had gone there?" Mama muses. "You would've *hated* it! No rowing team, nothing to do with water, only suburban football teams and cheerleaders."

"Rugby," I correct her.

"Meatheads, anyway," Kasia adds and smirks. "And all the arts programs, yuck. Meatheads in Birkenstocks."

We laugh. A passing suit grins at us, peering over rimless spectacles. "Babcia has your back," Kasia says, and points upwards with an index finger. "She had a different plan for you all along."

Mama looks at Kasia with amazement, and breaks into a smile. Kasia is wearing the yellow polka-dotted and ruffled dress that Babcia thrust on me for the Pope's visit. It looks cool layered on top of skinny blue jeans and high-top Converse sneakers. Kasia has more style and chutzpah than most adults.

WE HAD JUST graduated from Finch Valley Middle School when Babcia's sister, Ciocia Fela, called with the news that finally shattered our sorry excuse for a family. Mama collapsed on the kitchen floor, catatonic, and weighing more than all of us put together. She hung onto the phone receiver like it was Babcia's hand, and couldn't replace it in its cradle. She didn't fight when we undressed her and put her to bed.

I wasn't ready for Babcia's death, convinced that with her verve and persistence, and my brokenness and premature development, she would outlive me. Easy.

Kasia's breakdown was next, her pinching everything and anything she could shove into one of the ten pockets of her cargo shorts: mascara, lipstick, gum, cigarettes. It was only when she started smoking in the backyard, inhaling the stolen cigarettes all the way into her pelvis like Babcia used to, that Serge seethed. "I never asked to be anyone's goddamned father!"

"No one's asking you to be their father!" Mama yelled, and

hurled a crystal vase at his head. Crystal going through a glass-fronted kitchen cabinet on a hot June afternoon is a thing to see, so deafeningly loud, rubble and glass exploding and sparkling like New Year's confetti. It was the longest day of the year: an overexposed kind of sunny that at once made everything extra sharp and unreal.

When he launched himself at Mama, I got in his way and I actually did it. I punched Serge in his bespectacled mug, shattering his glasses with my fist. There was blood on his white beard and little green spots in my vision. The rest is as hazy as a Toronto summer's day. I do know the cops came, and I went to Al's.

"Imagine if all that hadn't happened," Mama now says, and gestures for me to sit on a plastic patio chair. "I would not have gone back to school, you might have—"

"Beer?" I interrupt.

"What about your flight tonight?"

"I'll have a beer," Kasia says.

Mama looks at Kasia like she is a talking cat. To me, she says, "Have you packed yet?"

"Live a little," I tell Mama, and put my arm around Kasia. I study the chalkboard menu of on-tap offerings. "As if you didn't have your first beer when you were thirteen."

"First of all, that's none of your business, and second of all, who are you and what have you done with my training- and protein-obsessed daughter?" Mama says. "Three cranberry and sodas," she tells the miniature server with pigtails.

Mama is right. Mama is always right. She has graduated from teacher's college and has lined up a full-time position at my high school, just in time to have the whole place to herself. Kasia will be going to an alternative school downtown. Mama has bought herself a gym membership and sometimes jogs by the lake, especially when I have races in Toronto. She's experiencing a renaissance, going back to *Ewa*, moving away from *Eee-va*.

193

The only person doing housework at our place nowadays is our occasional cleaning lady, Oksana. I remember being horrified and embarrassed when Mama first brought the young Russian woman to our two-bedroom apartment. "I'm paying it forward," Mama said, in response to the stupid look on my face. "Oksana is new to this country and grateful, like I was, for any work and any cash she can get." I would add my own sporting-goods-store-earned twenty dollars to the twenty Mama would leave on the kitchen counter in an envelope marked *Спасибо*: Thank you.

"Beautiful cranberry," Mama says to the server, and hands us our ruby-coloured drinks. "*Nazdrowie.*"

We clink glasses.

"Cheers!" Kasia hits my glass so hard it's a miracle it doesn't shatter. She smiles sheepishly. "If you make the Olympic team—"

"—*When* I make the Olympic team."

She grins. "Right—*when*—won't you be torn?"

"What should I be torn about?"

"Well, what if it's the Polish Olympic team that you make? You won't go back there or anything, will you?"

I've received an academic scholarship to study Marine Biology in September at the University of Victoria. Even though it's not an athletic award, I am going there primarily to row. Science I can study anywhere. I'm going west, not east.

"It won't be the Polish team," I say. "I promise you."

"Why not?" Mama asks, clearly offended.

I shrug. "Shit chances at a medal."

Mama slaps me on the arm. I know it's supposed to be a light, playful slap, but somehow it stings. I rub my arm and Mama goes to the washroom. When she's out of sight, Kasia says, "But seriously?"

"I'll row under that bridge when I come to it, but in the meantime yes, seriously. Not the Polish team."

"Really?"

"Really."

"Even if Poland had a good rowing team, you wouldn't want to represent your motherland?"

"Motherland shmotherland. I'm not going back there. Not even for a medal. I'm going west," I say, and force a big smile.

"Go west, young man," Kasia sings, and spreads her arms wide, nearly knocking over all three glasses. She suddenly stops and stares at me intently.

"You know, not wanting to go back there doesn't make you a bad person." We sit for a while in silence, contemplating what Kasia has said.

Mama, who's back from the washroom, watches me.

I nod absentmindedly. I expect Mama to give me a dirty look, but she doesn't. She looks more sad than disappointed that her eldest has cut herself off from her roots. I remember Babcia once telling me while trimming my mass of shaggy curls in the kitchen that it's possible to cut off my forked split ends but not to remove the roots and give me different hair.

"You feel what you feel: Canadian. It's good," Kasia says. She pauses. "You're definitely not Polish anymore, just your own weird hybrid."

WE WENT BACK to Poland for Babcia's funeral in June 1991. There was no one to pick the three of us up from the airport in Warszawa. There were only frenzied strangers: elbowing, negotiating, smoking. Kasia became one of them and led the way. She elbowed through the terminal, lugging the same old borrowed suitcase. Mama and I followed, large knapsacks on our backs, soldiers on a mission.

"Tata could have picked us up," Kasia said through the roar of the crowds.

"He could have picked *you* up," Mama said, wheezing slightly. "What about me?"

Kasia pouted, and continued marching forward.

I realized in that crowd, as a man rolled his suitcase over my feet as if they were concrete, how little was left for us in Poland. Here was all of Mama's money at work, her entire life's savings, wasted on bringing us back to this place to see Babcia buried. What was the sense in that? Suddenly I was filled with Boeing-sized anger and marched so fast Mama was left lagging behind. I thought about how now that Babcia was gone the main bridge between us and the rest of the family had collapsed. There was no one to summon crazy Wujek Kamil and his large car, no one to organize reunion dinners with devout aunts and uncles, no one to wave manically in the waiting area beyond the baggage carousels. And now that all the money was gone, what would happen next? What would happen to us in Canada?

We took a train to Gdańsk, a rusted green car that had obviously been operational since the War. Smoking compartments exhaled blue haze as we passed them on the way to the dining car, little more than a canteen. That democratic supposedly free Poland was still the same outward Poland to me, minus Babcia and Dziadek. The militia could have marched onto the train at any moment, carded everyone and hauled a few people off in dark vans with prison-like mesh on the windows. The only difference seemed to be that the acid-washed jean-wearing young men in the canteen car who would have been arrested for being young and potentially rowdy at demonstrations were now inhaling colourfully packaged M&Ms, Coke and Pringles instead of eating butcher-paper wrapped bologna sandwiches and hardboiled eggs and downing half-litre bottles of beer. Kasia wanted fries, but I insisted on cabbage rolls. Mama wasn't hungry. We washed the lukewarm meal down with my favourite Polish carbonated apple-mint drink. I took a couple of bottles back to our compartment. The few Canadian dollars we had converted into złoty at the train station bought us a lot of food. "Who knew you were so sentimental," Kasia mocked as we tumbled through the train with our loot. "Scarfing down gołąbki and squirrelling away Polish pop."

Mama was staring out the window when I slid the glass compartment door open with a suck and a pop. We didn't have a sleeper, but there were no strangers travelling with us. I napped with my head on one of the giant knapsacks and my feet stretched out on the opposite seat where Kasia was reading *Sweet Valley High*. The chug of the train and the bubbles in my belly lulled me to sleep. Walls laden with graffiti whizzed by. Laundry flapped. Church spire after church spire. I had terrible dreams that night, a dark, heavy sleep. I was deep underground somewhere, burying small animal skeletons and human skulls. Kasia woke me. The train had stopped in a black field. She was ranting about gypsies robbing us in our sleep. Apparently, I had been twitching. The compartment was liquid dark with shiny edges. I checked the door; it was locked.

"It's locked," Mama said. She scared the bejesus out of me. She was awake and just sitting there like a burned out lamppost, in the corner, in the dark. "Gypsies don't have money to ride trains. They wait instead on train platforms to see what each train that rolls by has in store for them."

When I fell asleep again, spooning Kasia this time, her sharp elbows jammed into my ribs, the dreams became more recognizable. Recollections instead of hallucinations. I was back in Poland, in Oliwa. It was Good Friday and I was lumbering behind speed-walking Babcia to the Cathedral for the Stations of the Cross. This wasn't a dream—this actually happened. She pointed to the fenced-in cathedral cemetery, and said, "There's our spot."

Creepy, I thought. "You have a *spot*?"

"Of course we have a spot," Babcia said, as if this were as obvious as a Canadian vacation turning into a permanent move. "We have a home for this life, and we have a home for the next life."

I shrugged like it didn't matter, but I still found it creepy. That kind of readiness egged death on.

"You know," Babcia once said to me with that uncertain look she sometimes mustered, "sometimes I wish I weren't Roman Catholic, so I could be cremated instead of being buried."

I coughed like I had just inhaled too much frankincense. My mouth hung open so low that I could've swallowed an entire censor of smoking herbs. "That's terrible," I finally managed. "To be *burned*?"

"No it's not," Babcia said. "You could be cremated and your ashes scattered into the beautiful blue sea, instead of rotting, petrifying in the earth, forever."

I hadn't thought about it that way.

"I know Jesus could," Babcia continued, "but there is no way I'll be resurrected anyway, with all the sins I've committed, with all the bad shit people do to one another."

Other kids might have been shocked to hear their grandmother say a bad word like shit, but I wasn't fazed. Babcia didn't knit, and she baked without recipes, her pastries as different as her moods.

"I'll just remain in the ground, forever tortured by worms and the elements," Babcia continued.

It was shocking, this strange desire of hers to be set ablaze.

"I'm sure Jesus did bad shit," I said, "and he was resurrected."

Now Babcia's mouth hung open. "Absolutely not," she said sternly. "The son of God? Doing bad shit? There is no possible way."

Babcia had a very different idea of saints than I did. In my mind, Babcia was not only certain to resurrect, maybe she might even be reincarnated.

And as Kasia, Mama and I were clambering off the smelly train at the main station in Gdańsk, groggy and paranoid, instructed by the conductor to keep an eye on our stuff and out of the hands of the persistent gypsies who were as foreign to me as brand names and democracy were to Poland, I wished Babcia were there to wave to us, to hug and kiss us, to feed us doughnuts and ham sandwiches in the car on the way back to her apartment. Even Mama looked uncomfortable and nervous. Had she never taken the train before?

A woman wearing colourful skirts layered one on top of the other and beads the size of plums around her neck begged for money. She held a baby under her arm like a football. "So this is freedom," Mama said to us in English. I handed the gypsy woman some Canadian quarters that were jingling in my pocket, before Mama could stop me. The gypsy shook them in her hand, a baby rattle held above her head, mumbling angry things in a strange language that sounded similar to French. So I handed her my last bottle of apple-mint drink. She took it and ran off, hissing like the train. Mama told me to keep my hands in my pockets and to never engage with beggars.

Before we went to the apartment in Oliwa, which Mama still had keys for, I wanted to go somewhere else first. "Do you really think that's a good idea?" Mama said. I popped my head into a blue Peugeot taxi the size of the train washroom. "How much to Morena?" I mustered in accented Polish.

Kasia elbowed me. I retreated from the taxi like a scared turtle. "What the hell for?" she whispered. "We're supposed to go to Babcia and Dziadek's, *now*."

"Shhh," I elbowed her back. "For old time's sake, to see how it's changed."

Mama said, "Speak Polish. If he hears English he'll know we're foreigners and we'll get foreigner prices."

The three of us piled into the back seat, this time with Kasia in the middle.

I had never been in a Polish cab before. It smelled like cigarette smoke on a rainy day and clothing worn too many days in a row.

"What's in Morena?" the old cab driver with hands like

workman gloves asked.

"Family," I told him.

Mama looked at me weird.

Kasia sat with her arms crossed and pouted. "No there isn't," she whispered in English. "There isn't even family in Oliwa anymore."

The cabbie grinned like we had just told him a joke about a Russian, a German and a Pole, but all we had done was give ourselves away. "You girls sisters? American? Have Polish family?" he asked.

Mama smiled faintly. As if she were my sister. "We're from here," she said, and crossed her arms a little too quickly and too firmly.

"Me, I'm part Russian, part Ukrainian," he said, "with Polish family." More grinning, while honking and cursing at a car trying to merge into our lane.

Ukraine: Chernobyl. All I could think of were charred trees, concrete as wide as the camera lens could capture, kids sticky with snot and that blood-red antidote we had to drink at school after the reactor exploded.

"That's nice," Mama said.

I wished I could talk with the cabbie in Polish as easily as Mama could. While my English was becoming nearly accent-free, my Polish words were disappearing as quickly as our family members. I was a foreigner, a floater, but most of all a fake, from neither here nor there, somewhere in between, somewhere in the middle, nowhere really. There was no place where I was just like everyone else. I was incapable of blending in, even in the place that birthed me. When my friends would tell me, "I'm a quarter English, a quarter Irish, a quarter this, a quarter that…" I always responded, "I'm one hundred percent Polish," except when Justin Shit would ask me what giant planet I was from. Then I'd tell him to fuck off. In that taxi, a day before Babcia's funeral, I no longer felt one hundred percent anything. I was a pile of sand, millions of grains of indistinct matter. I thought, *Is that what Canadian is?*

The cabbie let us out at the top of the street where all buses in Morena converged. He shouted through the rolled-down window, "*Dowidzenia!* Leave some dollars behind for us poor bastards." He exhaled blue cigarette smoke.

Mama waved him off, sour-faced. "Where to now?" she said to me.

"We shouldn't be here," Kasia said, and she pouted some more.

I wanted to snap at her and say, 'Where *should* we be?' but I didn't, because I partially agreed. I felt the same odd combination of attraction and disgust for Morena that I had felt when I was little, looking at my ripped up kitten after the Doberman attack. I wanted to bury the cat in the churchyard so badly, never look at her again, have someone else—a higher power—watch over her, but I couldn't stop studying her bright wounds.

Morena looked like her old self, familiar yet strange, kind of like Mama in those first moments we had glimpsed her at Pearson Airport. The subdivision was now a different colour—green instead of grey—shrouded by unruly bushes and trees that seemed to have grown disproportionately large in the previous three years, as if it had rained nonstop since we left. I navigated Morena's streets effortlessly, surprising myself that I could, despite all the surface changes, remember where to go. I could feel Mama's gaze on me from time to time, impressed with my leadership and stubbornness. She's the kind of person who can appreciate stubbornness.

The streets seemed shorter, everything more compact, buildings squatter and narrower than before, hidden behind the matured greenery. I felt enormous in those tiny streets. Maybe Justin was right: I was a giant from another planet.

Shops that hadn't been there before dotted the main thoroughfare, neon signs and English words advertised American and Western European junk food, cigarettes and beer. The large apartment blocks were not the behemoths I remembered. When they emerged from behind the trees though, they were still stark and grey. Now large black cracks in the concrete slabs made up the stories of each building. Some cracks had been patched with tar, forming webs that looked like cheap Hallowe'en decorations. I wondered whether the cracks had always been there and I just hadn't noticed them before.

Kasia and I stood at the top of the steeply down-turned Piecewska Street, a street sign proclaiming it now Popiełuszko Road. Our old apartment building was crouched at the bottom, at the end of the drive. My heart sank, falling right through me and hitting the asphalt below. It was so ugly, so Eastern European, so like the news footage on the CBC, of East Berlin after the fall of the Wall, so like the *Globe and Mail* photos of apartments in Moscow during all of Gorbachev's reforms. There it was: our Communist blok, like before. No change, except for the spider webs. I wasn't sure anymore what I had expected. That they'd put a wrecking ball to every Soviet housing project after people cast their ballots on June 4, 1989, and Solidarity came out victorious? That they had built bungalows for each family, level and compact, like in North York?

"It's so weird," Kasia said. "I don't remember living here at all."

"Want to go in?" Mama asked.

Kasia and I stared at her in horror.

"Well," she said, "what did you come for? To stare? This isn't a zoo. Come on."

She marched down the hill, taking small steps so as not to tumble down and end up face first in the rusted Lada parked in the circle. Mismatched laundry flapped in the summer breeze—not white and free-flowing like on the Mediterranean postcard Tata had sent once, but busy and crowded: red shorts, blue shirts, muddy orange dresses, a chaos of colour and style reminiscent of the former Satellite and Baltic States that now fly their flags at the United Nations.

"Bleh," Kasia said under her breath, following my gaze upwards to the many windows of the apartment block, shielding her eyes from the sun.

Since our apartment had never really belonged to us, Dziadek sold it after Mama, Kasia and I received our Canadian papers. Both processes—the citizenship and the property sale—were expedited thanks to advocacy: a letter-writing campaign to the local Member of Parliament, the fall of Communism and advent of capitalism in Poland. "It's amazing how much can be accomplished because of democracy," Mama had preached.

"You mean, with connections as opposed to without," I said.

She had looked at me in a funny way. "Must you always be so cynical?"

Even though strangers had lived in our apartment for over two years, Mama had some bizarre sense of entitlement to it, to being allowed inside, to snooping around. "What are you going to do," I asked her in the clangy elevator, "beat down the door and barge in?"

We were all able to travel back to Poland and attend Babcia's funeral thanks in part to the apartment money. Perhaps Mama needed to pay her respects to that old door stoop before visiting Babcia. She had been away a lot longer than I had.

The elevator lurched, clicked and sighed as the door yawned open on the top floor. The hallway no longer smelled of pee but of laundry detergent; swastikas and swear words were still painted here and there.

Evidently Mama had planned to do exactly what I didn't want her to, but nobody answered.

"Thank God," I huffed.

"So embarrassing." Kasia nodded in agreement.

As we stood in front of our former apartment, the Kwiatkowskis' armoured door wheezed open and Piotrek's mom stuck her head out into the hallway. Her eyes grew big and wet, curious snails poking out of their shells. "*Gosiaaa?*" she said. She still resembled a Barbie doll, but a three-year-old Barbie doll now, not a fresh one straight out of a box.

"*Dzień dobry,*" I mustered. My tongue was doughy in my own mouth. My voice quivered and I was suddenly embarrassed and really, really nervous. I couldn't believe she noticed me before Mama, or commented on me instead of Mama. Gosia, instead of Ewa.

"Gosia, *Jezus Maria,*" Pani Kwiatkowska reached for me and before I knew it her bony arms enveloped my large body and she was kissing me, three times on the cheeks. "Look at you! I hardly recognize you," she squealed. "You've really grown into that body of yours. What a beautiful young woman you are. I knew you'd grow into your skin one day."

She obviously didn't remember that she had once called me a pervert.

Kasia got kissed as well and Mama was embraced for some time. We were drawn into the apartment and told to sit on the couch where I used to do homework with stupid Piotrek while Mama played bridge with his parents.

The next several minutes were similar to watching graffiti stream past a window on a Warszawa-Gdańsk train: frenzied yet hypnotic. Pani Kwiatkowska talked, asking a million questions of Mama, about her job, marriage, house, etcetera, etcetera, while my eyes darted around the familiar room, inspecting its contents. The apartment was exactly as I remember it that time Piotrek pulled my pants down. Frozen in time. Pani Kwiatkowska apologized for the state of the place when she noticed me surveying it. The living room was immaculate. The large living room balcony windows were bare. I crossed my legs and held onto my knees. She said the lace window curtains were in the washing machine, and something was indeed turning in the front loader in the bathroom. But maybe it was my stomach. I hoped to God Piotrek wouldn't come home.

"Where's Piotrek?" Mama asked.

My heart stopped.

"He's in Greece with his grandparents until the end of summer." Pani Kwiatkowska tucked a strand of blonde hair behind her ear, which was studded with a tiny gold cross. "It's too bad the kids won't have a chance to visit with one another."

My old school was visible through the naked living room windows, as was the church along the road leading to downtown Gdańsk. When Pani Kwiatkowska started gossiping about the other neighbours (Beata having to repeat Grade 5; Beata's mom, Pani Kowalska, getting crazier by the day; Pan Kowalski drinking his earnings away), I drifted off, staring at the view, thinking about how we should be in Oliwa among Babcia's things, not in this insane glass house high above the ground. My heart shrank to a dried up acorn. "I'm very sorry about the girls' grandparents," Pani Kwiatkowska said, and crossed herself. "Especially that Babcia of yours."

BABCIA WAS BURIED in the same spot she had showed me a couple of years before, the exact one Dziadek had claimed through the Bank. Mama said, "It's amazing, the Communists wouldn't let you own a home, but a burial plot could be yours for the right price." I don't know why I had assumed they would be buried side by side. Dziadek's body had been placed there a year and half before, so Babcia's coffin didn't have to be lowered very far down. There was a wooden clank when the two boxes met, hers supported by his, his nuzzled deeply into the muddy Oliwa earth. I had never seen a coffin before, and I wasn't expecting such an intricately carved and lacquered piece of furniture, a horizontal credenza, something to store dishes in, not a body.

There were so many people at the funeral. Some of them stood with their backs pressed to the wrought iron fence that runs the perimeter of the Oliwa Cemetery. Suits, skirts, hats, housedresses, high heels and flip-flops: all sorts of people, not all of whom I recognized. Those who looked familiar held our faces in both hands, worried our heads would fall apart like rain-soaked peonies. People whom we didn't recognize, whispered, "There are the girls." We were *the* girls, and they were just strangers. Mama's siblings didn't cry during the funeral, neither did Wujek Kamil. They all touched their noses with folded handkerchiefs sixty-four times, twice for every minute we stood under the fragrant linden tree, listening to the priest talk about Jesus instead of Babcia. The perfume of linden blossoms was Babcia's favourite scent. Mama stood with her arms intertwined with mine and Kasia's, her body sagging between us, a wet sweater on a clothesline: heavy and impossible to dry. "She loved you more than her four children," Mama whispered. When they asked me to throw a fistful of dirt onto Babcia because Mama was crying too hard to do it, I got so dizzy I thought I was going to fall into the opening face first. My fingers refused to curl around the soil, so I had to get down on my knees and scoop it up with both hands. That tipped the sadness out of my head and all the tears poured out. The only people who could stop that voluminous flow were my mama and my little sister, two slender females who, in that moment, had more strength than one large girl.

EVENTUALLY, THERE ARE no vacant spots left on the patio. We are packed in, surrounded by Friday night revellers. Even though there's no privacy, one finds seclusion in the noise of the crowd. Mama gives in to one light bottled beer. "Draught gives me headaches," she says. Our bottles clink at the necks. Kasia grins like she used to, when she was little and proud of herself. My insides turn warm and liquid with excitement about going west: university, independence, the Pacific Ocean.

I have no idea how to tell my mama and my sister that I love them: a lot. That they're a part of me, like my overdeveloped body parts are, and that I'm as grateful for them as I am of my own body, no matter how huge of an asshole I am from time to time. "You can crash at my rez whenever you want," I tell them. *"Mi casa es su casa."*

"Thanks," Kasia says, and beams some more. "We can all soldier-snuggle on your single bed, like in a train compartment."

Mama doesn't say anything, just smiles a sad crooked smile.

We drink. I cannot think of a circumstance that would allow Kasia or Mama the resources to travel to British Columbia any time soon, but the thought is nice. Their smiles fade as if they're considering the same reality, sobering thoughts mixing with the alcohol they swallow greedily.

BABCIA'S SISTER, Ciocia Fela, had cleaned the old apartment, changed all the sheets, and filled the prehistoric fridge with new, flashy supermarket items: Nutella hazelnut spread, Babybel cheese and Danone yogurt. She slept on Dziadek's foldout instead of at her place because she said she couldn't leave us alone with the ghosts, while the three of us took over the cramped living room.

Babcia's couch was uncomfortable for Kasia and me to sleep on. I wondered how I had ever managed to share it with Babcia. Maybe I wasn't as big as I always thought. Mama slept on Dziadek's old army cot. There seemed to be extra furniture in the teeny apartment, and with all of our stuff, the place was impossible to navigate. We shimmied and sidestepped around things, planted hips and shins into sharp edges, bruised. "If you rub it really hard," Babcia always told me, "the bruise won't grow." So I rubbed until I was numb. But two days later, my skin still looked like an apple that had fallen from the same branch twice.

On that first and last trip to Gdańsk I decided that forgetting was what would allow me to cope. Forgetting didn't affect the way other people saw me—I was still a giant freak—but it altered the way I saw everything around me, which was key when I was trying to stay afloat. Mrs. White had told me she understood why I hadn't spoken for the first year at Finch Valley: it was my defence mechanism, my body protecting itself from the shock of the sudden move. Humans are like fish that change the colour of their scales to escape predators; we choose to forget certain things in order to make our lives more manageable. Forgetting Polish made my English better, more effortless. Forgetting Beata made my middle-school friendship with Althea immediate, necessary, firm. You can't have your feet in two different places: one in Poland, one in Canada, because that's a massive step that will likely rip you in two. You have to pick one, forget the other. If you do that, you won't miss what you've left.

Kasia had called Tata when we were in Oliwa. "He is such a loser," she said when she hung up the phone. There was no answer at the number Kasia dialled. She had called Tata's only cousin. No answer there either. Then she called Tata's work, the shipping company he'd been employed by for his entire career. They told her he was at sea.

I wanted to tell her that I already knew he wasn't going to be there but I bit the inside of my cheek instead. I thought of David's words and I agreed that Tata was a total loser and I didn't want anything from him at all. Mama gave Kasia an I-told-you-so look.

The shipping company secretary told Kasia that Tata had boarded in Rotterdam a few days before and that he was scheduled to return from Hong Kong at the beginning of December.

"No chance we will still be here then," Kasia said, and looked like she was going to bawl.

"Six months only," I said. "He's taking short routes. He must be doing well for himself."

Kasia shrugged. It was a trivial comment. I too, felt numb, as if the lower half of my body were missing. I didn't care if I ever saw him again. He was not the one I would miss. He was not the one I needed to see while in Poland. Babcia was gone, gone for good, her things broken by Dziadek or given away by her children. She was not coming back. There was nothing left for me in Poland. It was not my motherland anymore.

MAMA SAYS, "I will drive you to the airport."

"Not necessary," I say, and give her a peck on the cheek. I give the apartment a last look around. Do I have everything I need?

"You've always been so independent, so capable." She stares in my direction, eyes out of focus.

"Mama, I could never have done any of this without you."

She sits on my suitcase, flicks the zipper pull tab of a scuba diving gear bag, inside equipment as new to me as the city of Victoria, as unknown as the Pacific Ocean I'll be investigating. A rhythmic snap snap. I realize I have only ever seen Mama cry at Babcia's funeral, which was so surreal it might as well have not happened at all. In real life, she's only shouted, screamed, been upset, but never cried real tears in front of me.

"How about we get Ciocia Jola to drive us?" I suggest, and kiss her again.

Mama nods happily.

Ciocia Jola lives in the same apartment she leased after quitting her job at the 'faux chateau.' We were the ones who followed her to the west end and moved in right next door. The company and proximity to Polish makes Mama more focused. Although Ciocia Jola doesn't have her own car, she does have keys to ours (Serge's old car, currently Mama's new car, Mama's only material victory from the divorce), which is nice because it's like having two parental figures to rely on for the first time in my life.

Mama sits up front with Jola. I know if I sit in the back

I will get carsick, but I don't want to speak Polish with Jola. I have nothing left to say to anyone here—and not in a mean way; I am so irrationally elated to be leaving. Mama sticks her head into the crammed backseat where Kasia and I share space with my stuff. Jola smokes. "Look at you," Mama says in English, "driving off to university in a regal purple chariot with your entourage."

"A chariot *and* a chauffeur," Jola chuckles. "Sadly, I left my uniform at home."

Kasia hugs the scuba diving bag. "Don't you think it's so scary, so deep and dangerous?"

"Hey, you just missed the exit," I say to Jola, who curses and swerves onto the busy ramp anyway.

Kasia and I hold onto the backs of the front seats and Mama throws her hands up, riding this rollercoaster.

EVEN THOUGH MAMA knows full well that she, Kasia and Jola can't go past security, she still argues with the airport employee to let them through. I watch her rigid body and pecking head and marvel why she'd waste this precious time fulminating while my flight is already boarding. "It's not like it's another country, for Christ's sake," she admonishes the young man in uniform. "You think we pose a risk because we're foreigners, don't you?" He says, "Ma'am," over and over until I pull her away and say, "Give me a hug before I miss my plane." I absorb my compact mama into my Jurassic wingspan.

When she's more limp, and warmer, I swap her for Kasia, who will not allow herself to cry. She tilts her head back and keeps her arms at her sides while I squeeze her. "Stop being a freak," I say.

"You're the freak," she says, kissing me on the cheek and ejecting herself from my grasp.

Jola stands on the periphery of our hurried goodbyes, her hands jammed into her trouser pockets, purse under armpit, as if she's waiting for a blind date on a blustery day. She waves and blows me a kiss, *"Szerokiej drogi!"*

"You only say that to car drivers," Mama says, but Jola pays her no attention, so Mama blows a kiss, too, and starts to wave. I'm already walking away. "Call us as soon as you get there," she yells, and tears make pale tracks in her apricot-coloured foundation. "Even collect, if you have to. Just call us." She wipes Kasia's tears with her own sleeve; Kasia swats at her hand and joins in the waving. "I'll pray to Babcia and Dziadek that you get there safely."

The three are still waving maniacally and smiling too hard as I round the corner onto the jet bridge, where I can finally cry my happy and sad tears in peace.

ACKNOWLEDGEMENTS

Writing is not an individual event. It's a team sport that takes the coordination, support, patience and love of many.

I owe a huge debt of gratitude to my incredible mentor, thesis advisor and friend, Camilla Gibb, for her instruction, guidance and confidence. Thank you to my first ever readers, teachers and critics—Tracey, Doris, Zvi, Lynne and Helen—who first gave me the audacity to write a novel, the tools to get the story down on paper and the support to keep going until it was told. I couldn't have done this without the honest criticism of Nino Ricci and my Guelph MFA classmates and instructors, who helped shape this narrative and polished this writer's voice. Thanks to Lee, Megan, Tanis and Jael for reading various portions and drafts along the way, even if they weren't appropriate for anyone's eyes but my own. I am also grateful to Jena for her friendship and literary advice.

I have to thank my brave publisher and editor, Beth Follett, who believed in this story and took a chance on an unknown.

For financial support, I must thank the Toronto Council for the Arts, Crescent School and the University of Guelph's Constance Rooke Scholarship.

To my dear friends—Jed, Miri, Jordan, Aviva and Shari—for making life sweeter and for calling me a writer before I ever could. And to my brother Ian for being my number one fan; I am his.

Finally, I would like to acknowledge the critical role my family plays in my life. To the Maksimowskas, the Gutwinskis and the Vallées: from sustenance and finances to love and humour, I wouldn't be able to function without all of you.

To my husband Alex: I love you very much. Thank you for always giving me the feedback I need, not the feedback I want, and for never sugarcoating it. I know my Babcia is elated that I have found you.

This book is dedicated to my mother, who was and continues to be the best parent a kid could ever ask for; my hope is to be as unconditionally good to my daughter as she has been to me.

JORDAN GROSS

ABOUT THE AUTHOR

Aga Maksimowska emigrated from Poland to Toronto in 1988. She studied Journalism at Ryerson University and Education at the University of Toronto. In 2010, she completed a Master's of Fine Arts degree in Creative Writing at the University of Guelph. She lives in Toronto.

For more information, go to www.maksimowska.com